Asa Bullard, Society Congregational Publishing

Incidents in a busy life

An autobiography

Asa Bullard, Society Congregational Publishing

Incidents in a busy life
An autobiography

ISBN/EAN: 9783337120184

Printed in Europe, USA, Canada, Australia, Japan

Cover: Foto ©Raphael Reischuk / pixelio.de

More available books at **www.hansebooks.com**

IN

A BUSY LIFE.

AN

AUTOBIOGRAPHY.

BY

ASA BULLARD.

BOSTON AND CHICAGO:

Congregational Sunday-School and Publishing Society.

TO ALL,

OF EVERY AGE, WHO HAVE IN ANY WAY

BEEN INTERESTED IN MY LIFE-WORK FOR THE YOUNG,

THIS VOLUME

IS AFFECTIONATELY DEDICATED.

CONTENTS.

INTRODUCTION.

MR. BULLARD has kindly asked me to write a few words which may accompany the book which he now sends into the world. An introduction seems superfluous. Very few men are better known in the churches and homes of New England than the revered author of these personal sketches. Far beyond the bounds of the states in which his life has, for the most part, been spent, and beyond the shores of our country, his name and face and work are familiar. He has had the great advantage of coming to us in our childhood when the mind readily gains impressions which do not pass away. Into my own boyhood, as I recall it, comes the recollection of the tall man with his white hair and sunny face, his genial voice and winning manner, with the wise lessons which he taught and illustrated in a way which was all his own. He had the faculty of saying things so that they stayed where he placed them, and not only preserved the memory of the man, but made his words a living force in the young life. Now, in the fullness of years, he still walks among the churches, and children are listening to a man whom their grandfathers and grandmothers knew and admired.

Mr. Bullard has already written a valuable book upon Sabbath-schools, their history and methods; a book rich in information and suggestion. It seems fitting that he should add to that another work which should give more of the man himself. Many will be glad to know of his childhood, of the things which happened to him when he was a boy, of the varied incidents which have had their place in a life which has been long and industrious and successful. All this can be found in the modest pages of this book. The man thinks aloud, and changes his recollections into words. The story is told in his own manner. Every one who knows the tones of his voice will hear them as he reads. Mr. Bullard always knew how to tell a story, and he has well used his gift in his own biography. All this will be manifest to those who turn these leaves.

As I have this humble part in sending the book on its errand of love, I am sure that I express the feeling of a great company of men and women in thanking the author for all he has done for generations of boys and girls and in asking for him many years of the same service.

ALEXANDER McKENZIE.

CAMBRIDGE, June, 1887.

PREFACE.

THE fact that the special work of my life has been in behalf of the young, and has been continued through a kind providence an exceptional length of time, rather than any thing of marked interest in my personal history, it is thought may justify the publication of this narrative. The incidents here given, it is also believed, will illustrate a somewhat busy life.

When my work commenced there were few persons who were laboring especially for the young. There were certainly but few who were honored with the title of " the Children's Minister." Then there were but few children's periodicals like *The Sabbath-School Visitor* and *The Well-Spring*. The latter was published every week, and came, as some children used to say, " Just as often as father's paper does." For years *The Well-Spring* had a circulation of over sixty thousand copies a week. From two to three hundred copies were taken in several of the larger cities of California and other western states.

Of course all this interest in behalf of the young, then so new, made a great impression on the minds of the children and youth of those times. Those children and youth are the men and women of the present day ; and the impressions of their early life are now constantly seen, and oftentimes in a manner to me very touching. I am frequently met at public meetings, and in my visits to the churches on the Sabbath, by many a one, even of gray hairs, who, with a beaming countenance and in animated tones, says : " When I was quite little I heard you at ——" ; or, " I always took *The Well-Spring.*" So that my presence, and even my name, is associated with the early life of many, and recalls scenes of their childhood.

The following extract from an article published in a Providence paper will illustrate this : —

In looking over the Sunday notices, I read that Rev. Asa Bullard would address one of the Sunday-schools in our city on the following day, and I resolved at once to see and hear him. For the moment I gave myself up to the recollections which

for long years have clustered in my mind around his name. Sweet, tender memories, with hallowed influences, brought smiles and tears alternately. More than
forty years ago, Mr. Bullard went to a little country town in Massachusetts to spend
the Sabbath, and was entertained at my father's house. The little girl of the family,
who had just passed her third birthday, sat upon his knee and listened with the
others to his magnetic words. . . . I have never seen him since, but so clear and dis-
tinct was memory's picture, that I half-fancied I should know him on the morrow;
and unlike most of my childhood's heroes, and despite the forty years, I recognized
him instantly.

Now may not the following simple narrative of my own early days,
and especially of the work of my life for the young, also recall, to all
who may read it, memories of their childhood and youth?

In 1876 I published "Fifty Years with the Sabbath-schools," a volume of 336 pages. This was not intended, as is stated in the preface
of that book, to be an autobiography, only so far as related to my connection with Sabbath-schools. "All that it attempts," it was there
said, "is to give some brief sketches of the earlier schools; the modes
of conducting them; some of the changes that have taken place, and to
present such incidents and illustrations as have fallen under my observa-
tion in regard to the various departments and agencies of the Sabbath-
school work, as will be likely to aid and quicken all who are in any way
interested in the right training of the young, or in promoting the more
earnest study of the Word of God." That volume and this, therefore,
do not, to any great extent, cover the same ground.

My most earnest hope is that some of the little incidents, even of
my earlier days, here given may afford, especially to the young of the
present time, lessons of both interest and profit. These incidents will
show them that I was once a boy, just like other boys, only, perhaps,
in some things a little more so. And then, when I have passed away,
may it not through this little volume be said of the author as it is of
Abel, "Being dead he yet speaketh"?

Under these circumstances may I not hope that my numerous
Sabbath-school friends, and also a considerate public, will judge kindly
as to the propriety of publishing this humble volume?

                                                      ASA BULLARD.
"SUNNYBANK," CAMBRIDGE.

INCIDENTS IN A BUSY LIFE.

CHAPTER I.

MY PARENTAGE.

THE following account of my parents is gathered mostly from a genealogical sketch of the Bullard family, written some years ago for the "History of the Town of Sutton," by my nephew, William Sumner Barton, Esq., of Worcester.

My father, Dr. Artemas Bullard, was born in Holliston, Mass., December 8, 1768. He was the only one of his father's children who received a professional education. In August, 1794, with a small stock of medicines costing twelve pounds, and under a debt of like amount, 'he commenced the practice of his profession in Northbridge, Worcester County, Mass.

While he was studying his profession at Oxford he became acquainted with his first wife, Maria Waters, daughter of Ebenezer Waters, Esq., of Sutton. They were married in Sutton, February 17, 1796. His wife died without issue about two years after their marriage.

December 6, 1798, he married for his second wife Lucy White, daughter of Deacon Jesse White, of Northbridge, by whom he had ten children, three daughters and seven sons.

Although during his residence of several years in

Northbridge he had established an extensive practice, he was induced by the father of his first wife, Ebenezer Waters, Esq., to purchase his large and beautiful farm in West Sutton. In 1805, accordingly, he removed to Sutton, and thereafter his attention was divided between his profession and his farm. He was about this time appointed, by Governor Strong, surgeon of the then local infantry regiment ; and in 1814 he was elected a fellow of the council of the Massachusetts Medical Society. He might have gained an eminent position in his profession had he given exclusive attention to it.

As to person, my father has been described as " somewhat above the ordinary stature ; of light, florid complexion, light-blue eyes, nose strictly aquiline, and, in short, as his contemporaries have said, a fine-looking man. He possessed ardent feelings and great energy of character united with a sound judgment. His integrity was proverbial, always doing exact justice to others, and expecting the same from them."

My father's death was occasioned by an accidental fall in his barn, and was probably instantaneous. It occurred May 6, 1842, at the age of 73.

My mother was born in Northbridge, May 5, 1778. She was a direct descendant, on her mother's side, of the sixth generation from her noted ancestor, " Sampson Mason, the Baptist and dragoon of Oliver Cromwell's army." Her great-grandfather, Hezekiah Mason, died in Thompson, Conn., at the advanced age of 103 years.

My mother died at the house of her eldest daughter, Mrs. Judge Barton, in Worcester, December 15, 1869, aged ninety-one years, seven months and ten days. Her son-in-law, the late Rev. Henry Ward Beecher, at her funeral thus spoke of her : —

To this joyful coronation our beloved mother has come. All the days of her appointed years — years full of labor and duty — are accomplished; all her doubts are dispelled, all her anticipations realized; all she hoped for in her long and noble life, and far more than human hope can ever aspire to, is now her portion. We come to shed no bitter tears; we celebrate a triumph, not a defeat; a life perfected.

Her children are gathered here with her more immediate friends and neighbors, to pay the last honors to her lifeless form. How sturdily, how nobly she lived! Feeble, tender, but how enduring! Never strong, no one would have marked her for a long life. Well do I remember her as first I saw her. I was then a lad in college. Even then I was struck by the energy of her character. I remember my impression then that she was weak in body, and liable to meet an early death. Who would have thought that she would survive that stalwart man, Dr. Bullard, of Sutton, so full of the capital for a long and sturdy life? In body, as in mind, she was evenly organized. Hers was the strength of tenderness and gentleness, but underlaid by a quiet persistence of wonderful force. She was firm and steadfast for the right, wherever principle was involved; mild and loving, but with fixed habits of belief and thought, which kept her firm and true, even to sternness when occasion required. God taught her! With her vigor of character it would have been easy for her to make shipwreck of happiness, linked as she was with that strong nature, her husband. It would have been easy for her to purchase peace by self-abnegation, by sinking herself, but she did neither. She made herself a power in her home, but she ruled by submission and love. She made her home a happy one; and a greater compliment can be paid to no woman. She elevated the name of wife and mother, by showing in herself what it was possible for woman to be.

Early was I struck with her devoutness, by the depth, the richness, and the reality of her religious emotions. The church was always her care. She remembered the pastor and his household, the school and the Sabbath-school. To the latter she was deeply attached, and often in the still hours of the night, when all the household were asleep, upon her knees frequently, and always reverently, did she study the portion of God's Word which was to be the lesson on the morrow.

Well do I remember, in a great revival in Sutton, when the last of her class of thirteen rose to ask for prayers. All had been prayed into the kingdom, and by her. We had a gospel in our home. Her presence was a long benediction. If each one of her children, those gone before and those now living, could gather with us to-day and speak of her life, each would bear me witness that however much we may owe to the school, to the church, to the seminary, to ordaining elders, to the counselors of our riper years, yet the secret, the root, the fullness of each life was in the teaching, the counsel, the example of this mother.

As age withdrew her from active duties of life, her piety became brighter and her conversation more heavenly. God calls some away in the midst of their usefulness; some he calls in what men say is "just the right time;" and sometimes he keeps people here just as we keep pictures in our dwellings, to look at and admire, for whole neighborhoods to look at and see what it is possible for life to become.

That is the best man who carries his boyhood farthest into life with him. And that is the best woman who can take her girlhood farthest into middle life and old age. This our mother did. Herself a venerable matron, she stood as a child among her grandchildren; she stood as a loving child in her Father's home; all whom she saw, or felt, or received, were God's gifts. She lived in the liberty of love — a child in the great house of her Father.

CHAPTER II.

MY EARLY YEARS.

I WAS born in Northbridge, Worcester County, Massachusetts, March 26, 1804. I was the third of my parents' ten children. When I was one year old, the family — my parents with their three children — moved to Sutton, the town adjoining Northbridge on the west. This was afterwards our home till, one after another, we left the paternal roof.

My parents, when they first established the family, erected the family altar, which was faithfully sustained to the end. The influence of that daily reading of the Scripture and prayer, generally both morning and evening, and the asking of a blessing and the returning of thanks at every meal, was most indelible. All these services of prayer and grace at the table were performed with all the family standing. To be sure, when we were very young they were sometimes, especially in the evening, rather wearisome to us little ones, and I well remember how I used to wonder to whom my father was talking, as he stood up there before the tall clock in the corner, with his hands on the back of the chair and his face turned away from all of us.

Then, in the morning, my father would read, sometimes, a whole chapter in Scott's Family Bible, with the Notes and Practical Observations. This, while we were quite young, was not a little tiresome. Scott's Commentary was then issued in large folio numbers. I can well remember how each of those large magazines looked, as one number after another, once a month or once a quarter, came to our home, and with what eagerness we all used to look over each new number. I now have them all bound in six large volumes of from six hundred and fifty to nine hundred pages. And I reverence them highly as associated with my early home, my now sainted parents, and the sacred family altar.

We were all trained, from very early life, to attend church. As we resided over three miles from the center of the town where was our place of public worship, father obtained a famous two-horse coach or carriage " for going to meeting." It had two wide seats and was open in front. And every Sabbath, rain or shine, summer and winter, this carriage, with father and two children on the front seat and mother and two on the back seat, and one or two packed away somewhere inside, would be seen on the way " to meeting."

And how well I can recall many of the scenes in the church, which would be very strange to young and old of the present day. The square pews with the plain board seats on hinges, which were raised when we " stood up " in time of prayer, and at the close were let down with such a startling crash and rattle all over the house. Then the ice-cold house in the winter, with no fire except the foot-stoves of the women. There were always two services, with an intermission of about an hour.

One of the older children, by turns, boys and girls, remained at home to take care of the little ones and have dinner ready when the rest returned. And we all learned to get a repast that the hungry ones were sure to relish.

Among the things connected with "going to meeting" in those early days that made a great impression on my young mind were those of the old stone horse-block, standing near the meeting-house. There was such an appendage to most of the country meeting-houses at that time. Many of the people came to meeting on horse-back, the husband and his wife, or a brother and sister mounted on the same horse. And the horse-block was for the special convenience of the women in mounting and dismounting.

The old stone horse-block to which I am now referring consisted of a flat stone, six or eight feet long and per-haps three wide, elevated several feet by smaller stones, and ascended by three or four stone steps.

On and around this horse-block most of the men and boys, professors and non-professors, and even the deacons, in the warm season and on pleasant Sabbaths, passed their morning between the services. The time was spent in free and lively conversation. All the men took part in the talk without distinction of rank or learning, and none seemed to feel the slightest embarrassment. Men who never could speak in the prayer-meeting found no difficulty here. Till I was twelve or thirteen years old, as there was no Sabbath-school, I attended, what I have since called, this "horse-block class for conversation," and the scenes there witnessed are more vivid in my memory than are any of those I have since witnessed in the Sabbath-school. I do not remember that the sermon or the subject of religion in any manner was ever made the topic of conversation. The news of the day, the cattle and farms, the state and prospects of the crops, the weather, the prices of various articles of produce, the character of neighbors, politics, the approaching election, etc. ; — these were the themes upon which the older members of the "class," church members and the uncon-

verted, usually conversed.   Never can I forget the
surprise and wonder those scenes produced on my youthful mind.   Such conversation on the Sabbath day !   How
could any good impressions follow the services of the
house of God ?

Towards night, or in the early evening of the Sabbath,
we children all recited the catechism and passages of
Scripture or hymns.

Now, wearisome as sometimes these Sabbath services
were, I would not for the life of me lose the associations
of " going to meeting " on that holy day.

Among the many little incidents of my early life which
may be of more or less interest, especially to any young
friends who may read these pages, may be mentioned the
following : —

The Blacksmith Shop.

My father had a blacksmith shop ; and sometimes when
not called away on professional duties, he would do little
jobs in this shop in the evening.   One evening, when I
was a very little boy, I asked him to let me go with him
and see him make nails.

He said I would get sleepy and cry to come back.   I
thought I should n't ; and so was permitted to go with
him.   He fixed me a nice seat on the forge, where I could
see him blow the bellows, heat the nail-rod red hot, and
then hammer out the nails.   It was real fun to watch him
for some time.

By-and-by I began to grow tired and sleepy ; and then I
wished I was back at the house and in bed ; but I did not
dare to say any thing about it.   At length father looked
up, and seeing that I was very sleepy and ready to cry,
he asked : —

" What is the matter, Asa ? "

I said : —

" I wish I was never made ! "

Father drew the hot nail-rod out of the fire and raised it as though he was going to strike me, when I exclaimed :

" I don't want to be killed, now I *am* made ! "

Then, with a hearty laugh, he took me home to mother.

The Big Cupboard.

BETWEEN the kitchen and the dining, or sitting, room, there was a short passage-way. On the right hand, five or six feet high, there were two cupboards, a small and a large one, with doors. The small one was about a foot wide, with two or three shelves, where small tools and all sorts of things were kept. The large one extended quite a distance back of the chimney. The door was about two feet square, with a small, heart-shaped hole near the top. Into this great space were thrown all sorts of larger things, boot-jacks, hammers, boxes, etc. It was a catch-all for every thing that any one wished to put out of the way.

One day the roguish little Asa had done some mischief, when his father took him up and put him into the big cupboard and shut the door.

A loud outcry was expected, but there was not a lisp. The parents and the other children waited and waited for some evidence that the little prisoner would understand that he was in solitary confinement as a *punishment*. But there was no complaint heard.

By-and-by the father opened the prison-door, and there the little rogue was, having the nicest time with all the " playthings " he found around him ! But when the light was cut off from the hole at the top of the door, the little prisoner began to beg to be pardoned out.

The Catcher Caught.

THE warm sun of early spring had begun to disrobe the earth of her winter mantle. Here and there around our home, in the yard and the fields, the snow had disappeared, and the fresh grass was just starting to view. The time of the singing of birds, too, had come, and many a red-breast, on every sunny spot, was seeking his food and filling the air with his merry chirpings and sweet spring carolings.

These welcome harbingers of coming verdure and flowers attracted my attention. I watched them; but instead of making myself happy with their lovely exhibition of happiness, I began to devise plans for catching them. With my little bow and arrow, and my sling and stones, I pursued them from spot to spot, and from field to field; and many a poor, timid red-breast did I terribly frighten. By-and-by my roguish ingenuity hit upon a plan by which I was sure I could catch them. My plan was, to set a small fish-hook, expecting that the unwary bird would pick up the bait, and in a moment be safe in my hands.

This cruel device no sooner entered my mind, than I hastened to try it. I obtained a small fish-hook, and began to fasten to it a little string. In order to secure it tightly I used my teeth. In this dangerous operation the string slipped, and in an instant the sharp, barbed hook, which I was preparing for the mouth of poor robin, was fast caught in my own. It entered into the soft and tender flesh inside of my under lip. The catcher was now caught, sure enough — caught, too, in his own snare, which he was setting for another! What was I to do? I could not remove the cruel hook. The barb, intended on purpose to fasten it tightly in the mouth of the innocent fish or bird that should swallow it, was firmly fastened in my lip.

With great pain and fear, both increased by the consciousness that I was receiving only a just desert for my intended cruelty, I hastened to my mother. She tried to remove it, but in vain. I then went to my father, with whose sharp surgical instruments I was painfully familiar. Those frightful instruments — the very sight of which made me turn pale and tremble anew with fear — father now took out and laid upon the table. After much suffering, the hook was at length removed, leaving in my lip a deep wound ; but a deeper impression was left upon my mind.

Years have passed away since that wound was healed ; but the impression on my mind remains like the deep lines of the sculptor's chisel upon the marble. I then regarded this occurrence, and I still regard it, as a deserved punishment for my intended cruelty. I learned, by my own sad experience, that what was to be sport to me would have been, had I succeeded in my cruel purpose, pain and suffering to those innocent and beautiful songsters of spring.

I trust this story of my early days may be a warning to all my young friends against indulgence in cruelty towards any of God's creatures.

My Spreading-stick.

ABOUT the time of the above event, when four or five years old, in hay-time, I begged my father to make me a spreading-stick. After frequent importunities my request was granted. The spreading-stick was made of a small sapling, three or four feet long, which had two branches

at the top.   These were cut off five or six inches from
the stick, making two tines, like those of a fork.

With my coveted spreading-stick I went proudly into
the fields, and followed the men who were cutting down
the tall grass into swathes, and spread the new-mown hay
in every direction, as I had seen others do.   And did n't
I feel smart as I made the hay fly !   I was doing a man's
work.

Well, many a boy knows that what is at first a play
may become work.   It was not long before I began to
find it so with my spreading-stick.   When it was found
that I *could* spread hay, and be made useful, and save
some of the time the men had to give in doing this work,
I *had* to spread the hay.   It was no longer play ; it was
work.   And many a time, when my little arms and legs
became tired in this labor, I wished I had never asked for
the spreading-stick.   And yet, this early learning to work
and be useful has been a great benefit to me in my after
life.

There was one very curious event in connection with
my spreading-stick.   My Grandfather Waters, of Boston,
used occasionally to visit his old home in Sutton.   In
hay-time, almost every year, he would come ; and he
seemed to find pleasure in assisting in the hay-field.

One day when father was absent, grandfather went into
the field with the men to rake up the hay.   This was
soon after I had my spreading-stick, and I was on hand
spreading the swaths.   By-and-by I went to the windrow
grandpa was raking up, and began to spread the hay out
again.   Grandpa saw me and said I must not do it.   But
my memory was very short, and soon I was spreading out
the hay after grandpa.   He then told me if I did it again
he should have to shake me.   It was not long before —

boy fashion — I was repeating the mischief. Grandpa saw me and started towards me, when the wicked little rogue threw his spreading-stick at him and then ran. But grandpa soon overtook me and gave me a shaking — not a hard one, but enough to cause me to go crying to the house.

The good old man was troubled lest I should go with a complaint to my mother, and she might think he had assumed improper authority over her child. But that child, young as he was, knew better than to go to his mother with any such complaint. He kept his grief to himself.

At dinner grandfather told mother about the affair, which I had not ventured to mention. Then to show her that he was not severe, he arose from the table and took me from my chair and shook me again! That second shaking I did not soon forget. It hurt my feelings more than it did my body.

Some months after this, grandfather died in Boston, and his body was brought to Sutton and laid in his family tomb, about a mile from our home. One Sabbath, after the family returned from meeting, and had dined, father and mother and one or two of us children went to the tomb. They opened the lid of the coffin to see the face of the departed. Father lifted me up and said that was my "Grandpa Waters." I asked if it was the grandpa that shook me. And when told that it was, I said : —

"Well, I guess he won't shake me again."

That shows how badly I felt, though I so richly deserved the shaking.

Sad Influence of a Profane Man.

In my early boyhood I was a bundle of nerves, — all life and spirits, — scarcely still an instant, except when asleep.

I was always doing something ; and of course frequently
things I ought not to do ; so from my earliest days my
life has been a very busy one.   My grandfather would
lose his patience when he found every thing he wanted out
of place, or rather when it was not to be found at all.   He
used to say : —

"Asa will make something or nothing ; " meaning that
I would not be one of your halfway characters.   Should
I live long enough, that saying may prove true.

Although I was always so full of mischief, yet somehow I always had friends.   My little pranks and constant
glee seemed to attract the notice and win the affection of
most of those in my father's employ from time to time.

About the time of which I am speaking my father
erected a new building, and among the men engaged
in the work, was a man from a neighboring town whom
I will call Mr. Pierson.   Very soon I attracted his attention and gained his love ; and, in return, I thought there
was nobody like my new friend.   Every moment of rest
and leisure Mr. Pierson was frolicking with me.   Such
was the mutual attachment between us, that his influence
over me was almost unbounded.   And it was a dreadful
influence.   Mr. Pierson was a man of no religious principles.   Without exception he was the most profane man
I ever knew.   He would hardly utter a word without an
oath.   His habit of profanity had become so inveterate
that it seemed almost as involuntary as his breathing.
The wife of a clergyman, for whom he was working at one
time, reproved him, when he pleasantly replied : —

"Why, madam, I don't mean any thing when I swear,
any more than you do when you pray."

My attachment to Mr. Pierson and my confidence in
him were so great that the influence of all the instruc-

tions of my pious parents was neutralized, so that I felt that whatever my friend did or said must be right and proper. It was Mr. Pierson's greatest pleasure to witness my cunning tricks, and he was constantly encouraging me on to deeds of mischief; and this was not the worst of his influence. He would prompt me to some wrong act, and then teach me to deny it, always presenting himself as a witness — a false witness — in my favor, so as to shield me from correction. Many a time did I, through this wicked influence, and supported by the false testimony of this wicked man, cast my faults upon my elder brother, who had to suffer the reproof which I alone deserved. This cruel, wicked conduct I should never have been guilty of, had I not been led on by one in whom I had reposed entire confidence — centered my warmest affection. Through the influence of that false friend I "was made to sin," as "Jeroboam made Israel to sin."

There was only one occasion in which I ever used profane language. The time and the spot are indelibly engraven on my mind. I was returning from school with my elder brother and sister, and was near home. All at once I began to utter a string of the most dreadful, wicked words, such as I had heard Mr. Pierson use. They were put together in all sorts of ways. My brother and sister were filled with astonishment and terror, and cried out : —

"Why, Asa! you will certainly go to the place of the wicked if you use such awful words!"

But I only replied : "I don't care! Mr. Pierson will go there too ; and I want to go where he does."

On reaching home mother was told what I had been doing. And never shall I forget the sad and painful expression of that dear mother's face. She did not scold me — she never did that — but oh! how tenderly and solemnly she spoke of the sinfulness of what I had done. And she warned me and entreated me never again to use such wicked words.

How fearful the effect upon me of that profane and wicked man! The mischief of his influence for those few weeks it took months and months of instruction and reproof and prayer to counteract. Oh, the guilt of making others to sin !

The habit of falsehood, formed under the influence of Mr. Pierson, continued till I was about seven years of age. I also grew fretful and would cry at every trifle. I thus became a trial and grief to my father and mother. When about seven years old, I came into the house one day and said to my mother : —

"There! I am going to stop crying and lying." And my mother, years after, told me that she never detected me in a falsehood afterwards. That shows that even children know when they do wrong; and that they can, if they will, "cease to do evil and learn to do well."

Fifteen or twenty years passed away, and Mr. Pierson became a reformed man — a vessel of the grace of God. Yes, this blasphemer was brought in penitence to the foot of the cross. His breath, so long spent in oaths, was now spent in prayer and praise. The remembrance of his influence over me — that he had made me to sin — was to him a source of the most bitter sorrow and remorse. He often expressed a desire, as I was told, once more to see me ; but we have never met, nor shall we meet again, till we meet at the judgment bar. Many years ago he finished his earthly course.

The Famous Wind-mill.

My father had a large head of cattle, oxen, cows, horses, sheep, etc. It was no small affair to pump all the water these thirsty creatures needed. One of us boys always had to go home from school at noon in the winter three quarters of a mile to pump that huge trough full of water. It used to take about half an hour of the most laborious pumping to fill it. And this had to be done at least three times every day.

The subject of some easier way of doing this was often discussed. The plan finally adopted was to place on the barn, directly over the pump, a wind-mill. It was a most thoroughly made piece of machinery, with six large arms. Most of the time, when set to work, it performed its task admirably, just like a thing of life. With an ordinary wind it would fill the trough in a few minutes. Then the handle of the pump, to which the distaff was attached, was chained down, and the mill was quietly at rest.

But when there was a brisk wind, it would often throw the water from the top of the pump to the top of the barn, and pump the well dry in a few moments. And sometimes it was not an easy thing to chain the giant. Father would have to go up a ladder on the barn, get upon the trundle-head, and by means of the weatherboard turn the mill round against the wind and chain one of the arms. This was a somewhat daring and dangerous business. We were often not a little frightened at the furious antics of this monster; but no measures were taken to abate the cause of our alarm till after the great gale on the seventeenth of September, 1815.

In that gale the mill broke loose, broke off the distaff connected with the pump-handle, and then, for hours, whirled with the most frightful velocity, throwing off one board after another from the arms. The people in the village, half a mile distant, could see the barn swaying back and forth, and expected every moment that mill and barn and all would go to ruin. Father went into the stable right under the wind-mill, to get out a horse, when a board from one of the arms of the mill dashed through the barn directly over his head. The next summer, in mowing one of the fields an eighth of a mile distant, boards were found driven into the ground, thrown off from the windmill. Had it not been for the heavy rain that accompanied the gale, the velocity of the mill, it was thought, would have set the barn on fire.

This was the death-struggle of the famous wind-mill. It was taken down ; and we boys were quite willing to go back to the old hand-pumping, rather than risk any more such occasions of terror.

Stricken Down by Lightning.

In my early boyhood, one sultry summer day, there was a fearful thunder-shower. The lightning struck several times near our house. By-and-by there was a terrific bolt that ran down a conductor, tearing up the flag-stones at the back side of the house. My mother and myself were prostrated by the shock. The effect of that scene was such that, till I left my home for college and got away from the associations of that event, I trembled with fear on the approach of a thunder-shower, and, during its continuance, would hide away in some corner and cover my head and quake with terror. And even through life I have felt much as the little girl did, who was told that the " thunder was God's voice ;" she put her hands to her ears and, looking up imploringly, said : " Dear Father, please do not speak quite so loud."

I can sympathize with the little boy who said, after the earthquake in Charleston, that he was " afraid of the sky-quakes ! "

And then, the great gale on the seventeenth of September, 1815, when I was about eleven years old (referred to in the preceding incident), so frightened me that I have always rejoiced that my lot was not cast in those places so often visited with cyclones and blizzards and earthquakes. I often say: "The thunder-showers I like best are those that rain on us — and thunder somewhere else."

An Alarm.

In my boyhood I was, as it is called, very "unfortunate." Many were my disasters and "hairbreadth 'scapes." My accidents and injuries were so frequent that I seemed to become accustomed to wounds and bruises. And my mother used to say: "It does n't seem to hurt Asa to be hurt, as much as it does other boys."

When I was perhaps twelve years of age, my elder brother and I had just returned from school at night, and were attending to our usual duties at the barn. I was running along the stone walk by the side of the barn, to open a stable door, when a lazy old ox, for once quickening his pace to escape the sharp horns that pursued him, ran upon the walk, crushing me between himself and the barn.

As soon as I was free I turned and ran a few steps across the yard towards the house, and fell prostrate upon my face. My brother, not suspecting I was injured, called to me: "Come, Asa, get up, and not try to frighten me by 'making believe' that you are hurt."

But I did not stir nor speak. My brother then took hold of me to lift me up; and who can tell his alarm when he saw the blood running from my mouth, and found my muscles all relaxed, and that I had ceased to breathe? He hastened to the window of the room where mother was sitting with her infant child, and cried with a voice of agony : —

"Mother, Asa's dead! Do come quick!"

What an alarm to that mother! She sprang from her chair and, in her fright, almost threw her babe upon the floor instead of the bed, and in a moment they were at the yard. I had risen, and stood with my eyes closed, reeling as if half-asleep. I was led into the house, and after a little care and nursing was restored, though for some time it was feared the blood came from an internal injury. It was found, however, that it came from my mouth, which was wounded by the fall.

From the moment I was crushed till I was taken into the house, I was unconscious, my breath having been pressed out of my body. I felt, in recovering myself, bewildered, as one sometimes does when awaking out of sleep in a strange place. While unconscious, I was in a sort of dream and thought I was engaged in some amusement with my school-mates.

This event was the subject of much conversation in the family, and it produced, for awhile, a thoughtful state of mind with both myself and my brother. We felt that it was a very narrow escape. A little severer pressure, and I should never have recovered my breath. It was a solemn thought to us, that death had been so near us ; and to me it was doubly solemn, from a consciousness that I was all unprepared to meet the "king of terrors." Such a warning ought to have led me to make immediate preparations for the disasters of life and the solemn hour of death. But several years after this admonition of God's providence passed away before I was brought to cry: "My Father, thou art the guide of my youth."

Trifling with Danger.

THE autumn with its rich harvest had returned. The barns of the husbandman were well filled with the golden sheaves. In every direction were heard the quick sound of the flails that were beating out the precious grain, and of the winnowing mill that was separating it from the chaff and preparing it for the garner.

One day we were winnowing a large pile of oats. The machine was one of the earliest patterns — large, with wooden cogs, and requiring considerable strength to work it. My oldest brother and I turned the mill and father fed it. Long hours were spent in this fatiguing and monotonous labor.

To give a little variety, and to divert our minds from our weariness, I began, as I turned with my left hand, with my right to pull down the swift-flying cogs — a most dangerous business. But as I was sprightly and quick-motioned, for a long time I managed to catch them and escape the danger. By-and-by, as I pursued this foolish amusement, I became a little careless and inattentive, and in a moment one of my fingers was caught and crushed in the machinery. Although both of us were turning the mill rapidly, yet it was stopped the instant the finger was caught, as though it had been a solid stick or a bar of iron. A sudden change came over the feelings of that merry-making boy! The accident was so sudden that the finger was benumbed, and for a long time there was no pain ; but what a sight to behold ! — all crushed and mangled, with little pieces of bones projecting through the broken skin and flesh !

My father took me by the wrist and, holding up my hand, led me to the house. As we walked along in sadness, the broken finger was hanging down upon the back of the hand, and the dark blood collecting into the palm.

As we entered the house, my poor mother had another fright, and to the fright was added the painful reflection — and one that I had already felt — that this sad disaster was the result of carelessness and a very foolish trifling with danger. My parents used to say that I was always putting my fingers where I should not, and if there was any danger, that I would be sure to run into it, so as to see how it would hurt any one. In a few moments father's surgical instruments appeared, filling my mind with the most appalling apprehensions, and arrangements were made to amputate the wounded finger.

"O father!" I said, "don't cut it off; can't you save it? O father, I don't want to lose it! How badly it will make my hand look, and then I can not write. Do save it, father, won't you?"

These importunities of his almost broken-hearted boy led father to take a more careful examination, to ascertain if it could in any way be saved. The numbness had now passed away, and it had come to its feeling; and as father pressed the bruised, crushed bones and flesh together, to get the finger into shape, it called forth bitter tears and cries from the sufferer, and large drops of sweat rolled down my cheeks. Young persons may not be aware of the fact that a wound on a finger — on account of the great number and delicacy of the nerves in that little member, which aid us so much in feeling — is much more painful than one on the larger and more muscular members of the body.

A long and minute examination led father to attempt to save the finger. There was a large piece of bone on one side that must be removed, but it was too firmly connected with the finger to be removed at once. The finger was dressed, and after sufferings such as I had never experienced before, I was laid on the bed, with my poor hand resting upon a pillow. There I reflected upon the scene through which I had passed, and bewailed my folly, and, like thousands of others, made resolutions of improvement, only to be broken again when I should recover.

Every morning the wound was dressed, and new efforts made to remove the splinter of bone. These were seasons of great pain. Several days had passed, and the bone still remained. Unless it could be removed, the whole finger must be lost. I was so anxious to have it saved that I said : —

· "Father, if I am crying ever so hard from pain when you are trying to get out that bone, and you should get it out, I should laugh right out for joy."

The day arrived when arrangements were to be made for amputating the finger. Father worked a long time in the morning to remove the bone, but did not succeed. By-and-by I asked him to try once more. He consented, and after repeated efforts, the long splinter gave way and was taken out, and, while the tears were rolling down my cheeks and I was suffering the most acute pain, as soon as I saw the bone in my father's instruments I burst into a hearty laugh of joy: "O father! I am so glad! I am so glad. Now my finger will be saved!"

After many weeks and much suffering, my broken finger was entirely healed. The middle joint is now almost stiff, and is much larger than it ought to be, and the finger, though it was the longest on the hand, is now only about the length of the forefinger, and it has a large callous inside. Although somewhat injured in its appearance, and less serviceable than it would have been if uninjured, yet I have not a finger that I cherish so much as this one. It is on the same principle that the lost sheep, when found, is rejoiced over more than the ninety-and-nine that went not astray, and that one sinner that repenteth causeth more joy among the angels of God, than ninety-and-nine just persons that need no repentance.

In this incident we have an admonition against trifling with danger ; and we have, too, an exhibition of the enduring effects of a single foolish action. That broken finger I shall carry with me to my grave, a constant, ever-present remembrancer of the folly of my youth.

A Beautiful Vest.

I⊤ was very common, in my early days, for girls to braid straw for ladies' bonnets, and now and then boys would engage in the same work. My parents offered me all I could earn if I would spend some of my leisure hours, when out of school, and when my part of the "chores" were done, in braiding. I soon learned to braid, and it was not long before I could make my clumsy boy-fingers fly nearly as fast as the little, delicate, limber girl-fingers of my sisters.

After I had learned to braid well I could obtain three cents a yard for my work, and on one holiday, besides all my duties about the barn, etc., I machined my straw and braided eleven yards — thus earning thirty-three cents ! While I was earning this handsome little sum, many of my associates, who were keeping holiday at the town meeting, doubtless spent nearly or quite as much for cake and candy, and at night were not half so happy as I was. Their money had perished in the using ; mine, with its increase, was still in my pocket.

Among the many things that I purchased with my braid-money from time to time was what I regarded as a very beautiful vest. I thought there never was a vest that was quite as handsome as mine. And it was, in my eye, ever so much handsomer for having been earned by myself — bought with my own money. Why, I can even now remember just how that cherished, almost idolized vest looked ; those pearly buttons and those beautiful little spots of white and yellow silk all over it. I suspect, if the truth were only known, that vest sometimes caused my heart to swell with feelings of pride. If so, I hope long ere this I have repented of it, and that I now see the folly of being proud of dress, when even the poor butterfly — the creature of a day — can boast of a gayer dress than we ; and the lily of the field is more beauteously arrayed than even Solomon in all his glory.

In my early days there was very little done to train the children to give their earnings and savings for the benefit of others. There were no Sabbath-schools or societies to collect penny contributions to send good books and papers to the destitute.

If braiding straw were as common now as in my early days, how easy it would be for all children — boys and girls — to earn the money for their contributions ! But there are other ways of earning money now, so that all who try can bear a part in the work of benevolence. "Where there's a will, there's always a way."

My First Visit to Boston.

How enchanting are country scenes to city children ! Little do those brought up among them know with what delight those from the city look upon every tree and shrub and flower, upon every stream and hillside and meadow, in their visits to the country.

Then with what wonder do the children from the farms gaze upon the many beautiful and attractive things in the city! What a marvel are the splendid mansions, broad and pleasant streets, all smoothly paved, all kinds of stores and warehouses, with every variety of things for sale, all exposed so temptingly in the huge windows with their immense panes of glass, from the little candy-shop, with every thing pleasant to the eye and sweet to the taste of children, to the grand marble or granite warehouse, filled with the most costly goods! All these things are no doubt attractive to city children, but they are perfect marvels of interest to the children from the country.

Can I ever forget my first visit to the city of Boston, when eleven years of age? Oh, no! When I first came in sight of it, and saw in the distance such a pile of brick buildings, with the dome of the State House towering above them, and such a forest of church steeples and masts of ships, how the cold chills ran over me, almost as if I were approaching an army all ready for battle! When I entered the city, what a source of wonder were the signs! I could never cease gazing at those of the apothecary shops. Here was hung up a great golden mortar and pestle, or the gilded bust of a venerable man, perhaps of the apothecary himself. Then those large glass globes and tall glass jars filled with red and blue and green liquids, that I supposed were medicines that were exhibited for sale. Then here was a large hat, big enough for Goliath of Gath, hung over a store. Then there was a shoe or boot hung up, that would make a very nice dwelling for the "woman who lived in a shoe, and had so many children she did n't know what to do." Then there was a perfect model of a sheep, with a fleece of the whitest wool, standing all sedate and solemn on the top of a high pillar.

At another store were hanging out whole suits of clothes, coats, pants, and vests, with the cunningest little jackets and trowsers for boys.

"Father," I at length inquired, with the utmost curiosity, "father, why do they have all these things hanging up in the front of these stores?"

"These are signs, my son, of the things they have inside to sell. That great book, so richly bound in gilt, hanging over that door across the street, shows that that is a store where they have books to sell; and that large hat, big enough for a giant, is the sign of a hat store; and those coats and pants yonder show that they have men's and boys' clothes, all ready made, for sale."

"Well, father," I asked, "why don't they hang out a man to show where the lawyers are?"

Father said they might, perhaps, hang out a writ.

In this visit to the city how bewildering was the incessant and confused noise of the heavy trucks of those days, —on which they carried hogsheads of molasses, great bales of cotton and wool, and all kinds of goods, —and of all kinds of wagons and carriages as they were continually passing over the pavements! How the rumble sounded in my ears, for days after leaving the city! And what crowds of people on the sidewalks, keeping one on the dodge all the while, lest he should be knocked down and tumbled into the street. What a wonder this visit to Boston was to me! And what marvelous stories, of what I had seen, I had to tell my brothers and sisters on my return! How their big eyes did stare with wonder at the recital!

The surprise and wonder with which I gazed, for the first time, upon the marvelous scenes of Boston, were, doubtless, only what many a child and youth has felt on his first visit to a city.

CHAPTER III.

OUR NEIGHBORHOOD AND HOMESTEAD.

OUR home in West Sutton is a part of one of the most beautiful landscapes, of a mile and a half or two miles in extent, in the central part of Massachusetts. A former governor of the state once said that "the panoramic view from this farm was the most charming he knew of in the commonwealth." There is nothing magnificent or especially picturesque in it, but it is all lovely and beautiful.

From near the center, where there is a pretty village, it rises with a gentle ascent in almost every direction. The land is rich, and a large portion of it in a state of cultivation. The numerous farms are laid out in square or oblong fields, like patch-work, enclosed with neat stone fences; and when the various kinds of grains and grasses are ripening, it presents — with its border of woods, with Mount Wachusett in the distance, and its several small sheets of water, with the comfortable white farm-houses and their little clusters of out-buildings, scattered more or less nearly together over the whole landscape — a lovely view.

Our homestead, of one hundred acres, with its large, square, white dwelling-house, two barns, shops, and other out-buildings, is on the southern ascent of this landscape, a half-mile from the village, or, as it was called, the street.

Our mansion-house, which is a very substantial and still well-preserved structure, was erected in 1767. A magnificent elm, whose branches cover an area of more

BULLARD HILL
SUTTON, MASS.

SUNNYBANK
CAMBRIDGEPORT, MASS.

than three hundred feet in circumference, is still standing a few rods west of the house, and is one of the most conspicuous landmarks in the neighborhood, if not in the town, of Sutton. This elm, it is said, Rev. Henry Ward Beecher had in mind when he described the big tree in " Norwood."

It is gratifying to all the connections of the family now living to know that a considerable portion of the old farm is still retained in the family name.

But sin seems to mar and deface even the beauties of nature, so that we are obliged to exclaim with the poet, in regard to this neighborhood : —

> " Every prospect pleases,
> And only man is vile."

A knowledge of the moral aspect of the place at that time caused the Christian to view it with feelings somewhat like those with which he would have contemplated Eden, after innocence had drawn over her lovely face the veil of sorrow. Few portions of the state were more perfectly given up to intemperance and every species of immorality. Very few of the inhabitants for many years were professing Christians, and some of those few were no great honor to their profession. Few were the altars on which was offered the sacrifice of prayer ; and for scores of years a conversion was hardly known except in one or two families. " Like parents, like children."

Drear and desolate indeed is that neighborhood, however many its natural beauties and artificial adornments, where God is not acknowledged, and where intemperance and its kindred vices, like demons of night, rule over the people.

Many years ago, while on a visit to my early home, in conversation with my mother, the moral and religious condition of this neighborhood was considered. In this conversation we canvassed the state of the ninety-eight families that were located in an area of one mile and a half or two miles. And this was the result of the canvass: In twenty-seven of these families the parents were professedly Christians. In these families there were one hundred and twenty-five children over fifteen years of age. Of these, eighty-four, or about two thirds, were hopefully pious. Four were ministers of the gospel; five were deacons; and one was dissipated. In nineteen of these families, one parent in each family was pious, and all but one were mothers. There were ninety-five children over fifteen years of age. Of these thirty-one, or about one third, were hopefully pious; four were ministers; seven were dissipated, and the fathers of five of these seven were also dissipated. In fifty-two of these families — most of them residing in what is called "the street" — neither parent was professedly a Christian. Of their one hundred and thirty-nine children over fifteen years of age, only thirteen were interested in religion; and not one of those became interested till they had left the neighborhood and gone out from under parental influence and instruction! Twenty-five of these children were dissipated, and the fathers of thirteen of them were also dissipated; and all were in the daily use of intoxicating liquor!

I am happy to be able to say that, of late years, there have been great changes for the better in this neighborhood.

My nephew, Henry B. Bullard, who has a store in "the street," and cares for the "Bullard Hill" farm, in answer to my inquiries in regard to the present moral condition of that neighborhood, thus writes: —

At present our little church of seventy members is in a prosperous condition. Twenty were added by baptism about one year ago, and we expect four or five to unite with us next month. We have one of the best of ministers. The congregation averages nearly one hundred; and the Sabbath-school, of which I have been the superintendent for some time, about seventy; and it is in a flourishing condition. We have a Sabbath-school concert every month.

The old hotel has undergone a great change. The proprietors, who are very good people, have expended about $2,000 in thoroughly renovating it. It is in the best condition I ever knew it to be. If ardent spirits are sold, it is done very quietly. We scarcely ever see an intoxicated person here. The houses in the village have nearly all been painted within two years. I can not remember when the village looked so neat and clean as at the present time. No rough characters live here.

The buildings at the old homestead are running down. The house is in good repair, and only needs painting. Two winters ago, the ice injured the old elm very much. Several large limbs, two of them over a foot through and about thirty feet long, were broken off. We took off nearly a cord of wood. The farm is in good condition; the walls are all kept up. We have about a thousand apple-trees, which I prune every third year.

CHAPTER IV.

HOW WE CHILDREN WERE TRAINED.

SEVEN sons and three daughters, all to be educated, was surely no small matter. How to do it properly, situated as his family was, often cost my father and mother much anxious thought and prayer.

The village, referred to in a previous chapter, half a mile from our home, though beautiful and lovely in its natural features, as has been noted, was then morally one of the darkest spots in New England. Its tavern was the resort of the lowest class of persons in all that section of the county. The youth in the vicinity, instead of employing their leisure time in mental and moral improvement, were taught to waste their long winter evenings in the dancing-school and the ball-room, or in company with the vile at the tavern.

One would naturally suppose that such a neighborhood was a sad place in which to train a family of ten children. But my parents' puritanic notions of family government and their unfailing trust in God's promises to faithful Christian parents, and their wise plans for all necessary amusement and recreation for their children, were such that the influence of that village was rather helpful both to the parents and the children. It led the parents to see the great need of wisdom and watchfulness in their mode of family training, and there was before them all most affecting illustrations of the loathsomeness of intemperance and all its kindred vices. There were very few men and boys in that neighborhood who did not carry the marks of that low vice, and it was a warning to the children of the Bullard Hill Farm not to go in the way of the wicked, but to avoid it — to turn from it and pass away. They learned to look with pity upon those who were growing up in ignorance of their danger and wickedness.

Our parents regarded a wise Christian family government as the basis of all true Christian nurture. They believed that God had invested parents with authority to be used in promoting the good of their children ; that they were to use this authority " in the Lord," just as truly as that children were to " obey their parents in the Lord " ; that disobedience to parents and to all proper authority was also disobedience to God ; that it was much more common and much easier for an obedient child to give his heart to God than for one who is disobedient, ungoverned. So that parents should, in a proper spirit, use all the authority God had given them to prevent disobedience ; and if they did not do it, they would be accessory to all the sins that grow out of disobedience. And they considered disobedience to proper authority as the great, crying sin of the universe. It expelled the fallen angels out of heaven ; it drove our first parents out of Eden ; and it brought sin and all our woes into the world. Hence, in their estimation, no parent, to avoid an unpleasant duty, was at liberty to leave a child to grow up unrestrained and ungoverned.

With these views our parents sought to bring us up in the good old Abrahamic, Solomonic, puritanic way of obedience. Very likely many in our neighborhood thought we were brought up very strictly. But all we children knew about it was that there were certain amusements that the children and young people around us were accustomed to indulge in, that our parents did not think proper

for us; and so they would always provide for us some
other and safer enjoyments.

There were few families in which there was a more
delightful social intercourse between parents and children
than in this family, that others thought so strict. Punishment was very seldom found necessary to secure obedience. The reason was that we children early learned
that the only way to avoid it was by prompt and
cheerful obedience. This stopping to ask Why? when
father or mother gave direction we never dreamed of
doing. We learned that our parents' commands were
not arbitrary, but always designed for our good; they
were always right and just. The angels in heaven are
never heard murmuring and complaining of the commands
of their great Maker! Oh, no; they are ever watching
to know his will, and ready to spread their joyful wings
on errands of obedience and mercy.

With such a neighborhood as has been described our
parents saw the need of great wisdom in devising
plans by which their children might be kept from the
scenes of dissipation and rioting there indulged in on all
holidays. It would not do for them to forbid our min-
gling in those scenes, unless they provided some other
amusements for us more rational and more interesting.
Should they do this they well knew it would be natural for
us to become impatient of such restraint and to seek to
break away from their control.

To avoid this danger, and to gratify their own desires to
do every thing they could for our pleasure and happiness,
the sons of our minister and of several members of our
church and congregation, in town, were invited to spend
"election day," then the popular holiday in our state,
with us at our home. And what a day that was! No

pains or expense were spared to provide for us twenty boys entertainment and amusement. Father spent the day with us, keeping tally in our games, and now and then, as the game began to lose its power to please, suggesting some other, perhaps some game of his own boyish days. Was there ever a happier set of boys than were that day gathered at Bullard Hill? Our good mother entered into the occasion with the greatest interest. She prepared a rich and inviting dinner, with even more care than she would have done for the parents of the invited guests.

As each public holiday returned these boys gathered at some one of the different homes, till we were old enough to seek our amusements in social visits with our sisters.

Then, whenever the young people of the neighborhood arranged for a sleigh-ride with a ball, or any other amusements in which we were not likely to engage, our parents were ever ready to arrange for us a pleasant ride and a good social time in our happy home on our return. We all knew it was not the expense of an entertainment at some public house that our parents wished to avoid, but it was to shield us from the temptations and unhappy influences to which such scenes would expose us.

Now the result of this mode of family government and training was that all the ten children of this family united with the church, and all but one or two before they were of age.

Then we lived, as has been said, over three miles from our place of worship, and there was scarcely a family within a mile that had any sympathy with us in regard to the proper observance of the Sabbath. All this led us to rely upon ourselves for associates and recreation. It very early became our custom, thus isolated, for parents and children to spend our leisure winter evenings together, while some one read aloud an interesting and valuable book, in regard to which any one was at liberty to ask questions or make remarks. In this way, many of the most important works of history were read, and we became acquainted with the government, religion, manners, and customs, etc., of all nations.

This manner of spending the winter evenings had an important influence on our intellectual and religious character. A taste for reading and a desire to gain useful knowledge were awakened.

Our father had set his heart upon training his boys for the farm. He was hoping soon to be relieved to a great extent from its care by entrusting its management mainly to his eldest son. But his plans for the education of his children had produced a deeper impression than he had anticipated. Such a love of study and such a thirst for literary pursuits had been awakened, that my eldest brother, who, with my sister older, had just entered upon the Christian life, now expressed his wish to commence a course of study for the gospel ministry.

At first this was a great disappointment to father. And yet the conversion and usefulness of the children was the burden of his daily prayers. Father soon yielded his wishes to the indications of Divine Providence, and the whole family now became interested in this important object before them. Every one was ready to help by economy and in every other way practicable to meet the expense of carrying this son and brother through college and into the sacred office.

This brother used to say that it was our manner of spending winter evenings that led him to seek a public education. He often acknowledged with lively emotion his gratitude to his parents for the habit of reading and study which they taught him to form in early life ; and for the still more valuable habit of relating, in his own words, the narratives and thoughts of the various authors that were read together in the family. Whenever he returned home during vacations he helped to increase the interest among his brothers and sisters in reading and study, so that all showed an unusual attachment to books and a thirst for general knowledge. After a hard day's work on the farm, we boys would spend hours in reading and study, either alone or in company with each other and our sisters.

The result of our parents' mode of educating their children (if I may here anticipate a few years in my narrative) was that five of the sons commenced a course of education with a view to the ministry, and another would have been glad, had the opportunity offered, to enter upon the same course ; four completed their collegiate education, three entered the sacred offices, and three, other professions. The three daughters received the best education the academies of those days afforded, and all became wives of professional men — two of them clergymen.

The education of so large a family of course caused a hard and long-continued struggle and great expense on the part of our parents. But they felt that there was no investment they could make for their children that would be so valuable and safe as a good education ; and that there was no way in which they could receive so rich and satisfactory a return for all their labor and care as to see their children, through the qualification of a thorough intellectual and religious training, occupying places of honor and usefulness.

I can but hope that this narrative may be helpful to many parents who are inquiring anxiously, "How shall we order our children? How shall we do unto them?"

Children must have something to employ and interest them. Nature teaches that the young must have amusement, recreation; and no wise parent will leave his children to seek their associates and amusements without their aid and watchful care. Expense of time and money can not be more wisely incurred than by rendering such aid and care.

That the literary and religious tastes and character and subsequent lives of so large a family of children, so isolated from literary, moral, and religious associations and influences, should have been so much formed through the right employment of winter evenings, is an instructive lesson to all parents who would see their children growing up to be respected and useful in their day and generation.

Learning to Do Things.

As I have already intimated, I was brought up on a farm, and my father taught his boys to work. And not one of us, even those in professional life, has ever regretted this early training.

I had, perhaps, an unusual amount of natural elasticity. I was quick in all my movements, and on this account was called on more frequently than my brothers to do any thing that was to be done quickly — turn the grind-stone, go on errands, etc. It was : —

"Asa, run and get such a thing;" and though it was not exactly meant that I should *run*, yet my swift walk was very nearly that. A quick step, to the present day, has been my natural gait. In walking the street I seldom go behind any one, if I can get ahead. This is not planned or designed beforehand, but is intuitive. A slow step or a slow act of any kind is to me unnatural, and therefore more fatiguing than a quick one.

My father, when about twelve years of age, went to live some years with an uncle who was a blacksmith. His special duty for some time was to blow the bellows for his uncle. But he was a boy who always kept his eyes and ears open to learn all he could about every thing around him. In this way he really learned the trade of the blacksmith. He learned to do so much in this line that after he purchased his farm in Sutton he had a small blacksmith shop and also a carpenter's shop built, for his own use and that of his boys. He always used to shoe his own horses and oxen, making the shoes and nails, sharpened his plowshares, mended his chains, and, in short, did any thing in that line that needed to be done on a farm. He could also make a sled and shoe it, repair carts and all other farm implements. All this he would do evenings, or on rainy days when he could not work out or was not called away on professional duties. Knowing how to do these things not only saved him much time, but also much expense.

This habit of my father may have begotten in me my interest in the same direction. From my boyhood I had a great desire to do every thing I saw any one else do. I liked to spend my play-hours with the tools in my father's shop, making bows and arrows, sleds, boxes, etc., which I learned to make quite neatly.

In those days each family had their boots and shoes made at home. A shoemaker, or a " cobbler," as he was then called, came with his bench and tools on his shoulder, and spent days, and even weeks, making all the boots and

shoes for the whole family for a year. Those occasions
were full of interest to me. I begged the privilege of
going into the chamber with the shoemaker and learning
his trade. I very soon learned to peg and sew and make
myself quite useful in the work. To be sure, there were
times in after years, during my college vacations, when
my knowledge and skill in mending old boots and shoes
were of more use to the family than of recreation to me.
Still I have never regretted that I came so near being a
shoemaker.

I had a great taste for the garden. Raising all kinds of
vegetables, flowers, shrubbery, etc., was my delight. While
my brothers and the hired men were resting at noon-time
in the summer, I would seek my rest among my thriving
beds of beets and carrots, noting the growth of my
melons and cucumbers, and enjoying the varied beauties
and sweet fragrance of my roses and pinks, etc. And this
interest in horticulture has grown ever since, as every one
can see who visits my vine-clad home, in the midst of
choice shrubbery and ever-blooming flowers.

This knowing how to do things, which I so early learned,
has been an unfailing source of pleasure, as well as a practical benefit, to me all my life. For the forty years I have
had a home of my own, there has been scarcely a week, or
even a day, when my knowing how to do things has not
been of service to me. There is hardly any little repair
or improvement needed about the house but I can make
it. And while it is usually a pleasant recreation to lay
aside my studies for a short time, it is also an important
matter of economy.

I am told that a pane of glass or the cord of a window
has been broken; there is a hole in the bottom of a tin
dish or the handle has unsoldered; the pump, the clock, or

the lock on a door or trunk is out of order ; or a few things need painting : all these things I can usually repair and put in order, and do it in less time than it would take to get the glazier, tinker, pump-maker, or painter to come and do it, and at the same time save the dollar or fifty cents charged for every little job.   A new shelf or bookcase is wanted, or a trellis for my clematis, honeysuckle, or grape-vines ; I have a work-bench and tools in the barn-chamber, and some hour when I need relaxation and exercise the work is done.   My house needs shingling, or a new room is needed ; and, if I can spare a little time from my pro-fessional duties, I can turn my skill to account in aiding the carpenter ; and thus hundreds and hundreds of dollars have been saved to me by having learned to be my own mechanic.

Now, I would like to say to all boys : " Is it not worth your while to be learning to do things ? "   All may not have an equal tact or natural genius for turning their hand to almost every thing.   But every one ought to know enough, no matter what his employment in life is to be, if called to harness a horse in an emergency, not to harness him with his head towards the carriage, or to put on a saddle wrong end foremost, or to think he has done a smart thing by making a round button for a door, or by put-ting in a screw at each end of one that is properly made, as some men, with an honorary title at one or both ends of their names, have done.

While I would commend this subject of learning to do things to the attention of all boys, I presume the girls too may find it greatly to their advantage to be learning to do things in their sphere of life.

Three Hours in a Corn-field.

MY father purchased his large farm with special reference to the training of his boys. He believed the old adage,

> " Satan finds some mischief still,
>   For idle hands to do."

While ever ready to make ample provision for all needful amusements and recreation for his boys, as I have already shown, he believed that our good required that we should be trained to habits of industry. And we began to form these habits at an early age. When only six or eight years old, we were trusted with the responsibility of going to mill and on various other errands with the horse and wagon. We were known through the county, perhaps I may venture to say, as very smart, industrious boys. If a father wished to rebuke the idleness of his sons, or give them an example of industry, he would refer to the boys at Bullard Hill.

Some thought that our father worked his boys too hard; that he begun our training on the farm when we were too young. But a healthier, more robust, or happier set of youngsters was not to be found in the country. We all felt a personal interest in every department of work on the farm. We all felt that we had an ownership in it. We were ambitious to have the work of each season — planting, hoeing, haying, and harvesting — done as early as any other farmer in town. Whether father was with us or not, we were industrious; no eye-serving among us. We were in full sympathy with our father in every plan for improvement; and he always consulted with us, and carefully considered the suggestions any one of us might make.

The following incident will illustrate our ambition. Father was a practical farmer, and when professional duties would permit, he engaged in personal labor with his boys, as already stated.

One lowery afternoon in hay-time there was a good half-day's work for three men to be done in hoeing a field of corn. Father took three of us boys, the eldest about seventeen years of age, to do this work. He told us he would plow this field and then go to another, leaving us to spend the afternoon in hoeing it. This was before the introduction of the cultivator. Two furrows were plowed between the rows, one turning the earth towards one row, and the other towards the other row.

As father began the first furrow, one of us, without any preconcerted arrangement, began to hoe; a second boy went a third way through the field and began to hoe; and the other boy began at the other end as father commenced the second furrow. By the time the two furrows were plowed, the row was hoed. Then we commenced on the next in the same way, and with the same result. At this, father began to quicken the speed of the horse, and we, becoming a little excited, quickened our speed also.

Father's motto was, "that what was worth doing was worth well-doing;" no halfway work on his farm. So he several times said: "Boys, you are not slighting your work, are you?"

And several times he stopped to see; and finding the work satisfactory, hastened back and urged on his horse, to keep out of the way of these now thoroughly aroused and ambitious young farmers.

The result of this trial on the "race-course" of hoeing was that the work of half a day for three men was completed in three hours by three boys, and we left the field in triumph with our father !

This feat became known and was the subject of frequent conversation among the farmers all through the neighborhood. And father felt that the stock he held in his boys had suddenly gone up several per cent. ! He often described that exciting time in the corn-field with great pride and satisfaction.

Not one of us boys, though six of us entered professional life, ever regretted his early agricultural training. We were protected from the evil influences of idleness, and we all obtained a knowledge of "doing things," which has ever been of great service to us. And not one of us but has often recalled, with no small interest, the feat of those three hours in the corn-field.

Bullard Hill Farm.

SOME little description of the farm at Bullard Hill, the mode of carrying it on, and a few other incidents connected with it may be of interest.

As this farm was purchased, as already stated, with special reference to the training of his boys, father arranged and directed every thing connected with it to this end. Every field, for tillage or pasture, had its particular name ; and no resident in a city could be more familiar with the names of the streets in his neighborhood than each member of this family was with the location and name of every lot and pasture, orchard and garden, on the farm. There was the Long lot, the Sap-tree lot, the Cider-mill lot, the Blacksnake Den lot, the Spring pasture, the Oak-tree pasture, the Pennyroyal pasture, the Oven orchard, etc. Every rod of this farm showed the effect of wise and skillful husbandry.

We young farmers were taught that there must be no marks of slothfulness. Weeds and bushes were not permitted to get the upper hand. There were no unsightly nooks and corners. A proper care of the buildings and tools was taught. No leaving plows and carts and other farming utensils lying about the yard or field, to rust in the storm and burn in the sun. A taste for neatness and order was cultivated. Every thing must have its place, and when not in use, must be in its place. If a sprig of white-weed, or oxeye, as it was called, — which was the most dreaded pest of the farm, — was found, it was carefully taken up, the roots placed on the wall with a stone upon them, and the heads cast into the fire.

Father had various plans to collect and prepare large quantities of good dressing for his fields. He gathered muck from the meadow and the rich washings that accumulated by the road-side. He replaced old walls with bank walls, so as to get the loam under them for his barn-yard and compost heap, and at the same time improve the appearance of the farm. We boys all entered into the plan of saving every thing that would help to enrich the fields and make them more productive.

We were encouraged by obtaining the best farming-tools that were to be had, and raising the best stock ; and father would have been glad to have only the best help when obliged to have any. But many of the families in which he practiced were poor, and he had to take his pay in work, poor though that might be, or receive no compensation at all. He used to say there were three classes of the poor for whom he doctored — "the Lord's poor, the devil's poor, and poor devils." He was willing to help the Lord's poor, even though there was no prospect of pay. But when he came to the other two classes, and especially the poor devils, who would be sure to send for him on the most stormy nights and then never pay if they could avoid it, he thought that was a pretty hard case.

It is a great privilege to be brought up on such a farm, and by such a practical farmer. No matter what the profession of one is to be in after life, the influence of an early agricultural training can not but be beneficial.

With this large family of ten children to feed and clothe and educate — four or five of them to receive a public education — it cost a long and very earnest struggle to remove the heavy debt with which this fine farm was encumbered. Every child was interested in securing that end. But that debt was really a powerful and most beneficent educator in that family. It taught invaluable lessons of frugality, economy, and industry, which have never been forgotten. It inspired every one to personal and vigorous effort to have our home free from all encumbrance. And that was a memorable and most joyous day when that long-sought-for object was accomplished. The very thought of a home unincumbered with debt one would suppose would lead every farmer and every member of his family to the most earnest and persevering effort to secure such a boon.

A Present to our Minister.

A GENERATION or two ago it was common in most parishes for the people from time to time to make little presents to their minister. Not only on thanksgiving occasions, but almost every week some one would carry something that would be useful in housekeeping to the parsonage. It was not because the salary was small, — though it was in most cases small compared with salaries generally at the present day, — but it was an expression of interest in the minister and his work.

This practice, which was most happy in its influence alike upon the giver and the receiver, and which often-times greatly cheered the heart of the pastor as a token of confidence and affection, is not so common at the present day. The railroads bring every one so near the market that every thing he can raise is just as good to him as so much money; and it is a different thing to give the minister a present now and then in money from what it used to be to give a bushel of apples or potatoes, a loin of veal, a few dozen of eggs, or a few pounds of butter or cheese. And so these love-tokens to the pastor are comparatively few in our times.

Once a year, at least, a special present went from our farm to the parsonage. My father was famous for getting up a splendid load of wood, whether intended for a present or for market. Instead of arranging the crooked sticks so as to make the largest bulk possible out of the smallest quantity of wood, he either rejected the crooked sticks or made "the crooked straight" by cutting, and then pack-ing so closely that a squirrel could scarcely make its way through it.

At the proper season he put long stakes into the sled and made up a load of a cord and a half or two cords of well-seasoned hard wood that was fit to be photographed. On top of this load was placed a bag of apples from our fine large orchard, a cheese, and a few pounds of butter from mother's well-filled dairy-room, and perhaps a loin of veal or a spare-rib of pork. Then two of us boys, when not more than twelve or fifteen years of age, with a team of two or three yoke of oxen and a horse, would take this present, upon which our whole family had bestowed our blessings, to the minister. And did ever two boys feel quite so smart as did these young teamsters on such an errand?

As that splendid load of wood went on its way through the town every body knew where it was going, and we too knew they did.

On arriving at the parsonage the venerable and venerated minister, the late Rev. Edmund Mills, uncle of Samuel J. Mills, the early missionary (and ah, how plainly I can now see his tall, majestic, and gentlemanly form!), and his family came out, with their hearty thanks and "God bless you." The minister helped unload the wood, and we shrewdly managed to give him, when we could, the big ends of the sticks, that we might see the minister lift.

Was n't it a scene never to be forgotten by us? And did n't we and all the family who were at church hear our minister preach the next Sabbath? Did he ever preach half so well, and did we ever listen with half so much interest before? That load of wood as a present did the givers ever so much more good than it did the recipients. We all found that it was, indeed, "more blessed to give than to receive."

Every one is always interested where he invests property. This is a well-known principle in life. Hence the little boy ran with so much eagerness to the missionary meeting because, as he said: "I have an interest in that concern, for I have given a shilling to it."

Why do not parents more generally think of the interest these little attentions to the minister will awaken in their children and in themselves toward him and his instructions? Let the children have a part in these little offerings. Such presents from the people — though together they are important helps to the minister in his family — are chiefly valuable as tokens of confidence and interest in him and his work among them. And it would be well could this old custom be revived.

CHAPTER V.

MY RELIGIOUS EXPERIENCES.

I ENJOYED the instruction of pious parents and, from the age of twelve, of the Sabbath-school. Like most children religiously educated, I often had serious thoughts of God and the judgment, of heaven and hell.

When I was about sixteen my eldest sister was hopefully converted. For several weeks after this my mind was tender and my thoughts serious. In a few months my elder brother, then absent, became interested in religion. News of this revived and greatly deepened all my anxious thoughts. I now began to see the evil of sin. I often repaired to the barn and, throwing myself on the hay, poured out my bitter tears and cries unto God. The Holy Spirit was evidently whispering to my heart. Oh, that I had cherished that whisper as I would have cherished the last whisper of a dying friend!

I saw an awful division in the family. The parents and the elder brother and sister were on the side of God and bound to heaven ; the younger members, of whom I was the eldest were on the side of Satan and bound to the world of woe. One day I took my five younger brothers and sisters to my chamber. I shut the door, and there, amid sobs and tears that almost choked my utterance, unburdened my heart and told them that I was leading them down to the world of woe. This was a melting scene. The power of sympthy was so great that we all wept together.

Soon after this our indulgent father gave his sons a holiday. I resolved to spend that day in my chamber alone, seeking after God. Oh, how little, on that bright morning, did I think what a midnight of darkness I would soon bring over my own soul! I finished my few morning duties at the barn and was on my way to my chamber. The scalding tears were flowing from my eyes. As I passed near the shop I heard the merry voices of my brothers engaged in their sports. I hesitated. Conscience told me to go straight to my chamber. The tempter said: "Just see what the boys are doing and then go to your chamber."

I yielded to the tempter's suggestion and went to the shop. My brothers were making bows and arrows. I stood a moment and was just turning to leave when my eye caught a fine stick for a bow. I said to myself: "I will just shave out a bow, and then I will go to my chamber."

Oh, how conscience plunged her sting deep into my heart as I seated myself with the stick and the shave! For a moment I was ready to cry out with pain. Yet amid all this anguish of spirit I went on and finished a beautiful bow. Now I would go to my chamber. I hesitated. I wanted to see how it would look when strung. I knew it would be trifling with the voice of conscience and the Spirit to tarry another moment, but again I yielded to the tempter and strung my bow. After writhing under another sting from conscience, and trembling as it thundered in my ear, I seated myself to make an arrow, which should certainly be the last act of resistance to the Spirit and to conscience. Oh, how little did I yet know the power of temptation or of my own weakness!

My bow and arrow were now completed. I had thrice

yielded to the voice of the tempter, stifled conscience, and
hushed the strivings of the Spirit. With even less resistance than before I yielded again and accompanied my
brothers to the field in search of game. I would only
shoot once, and then return. But the tempter continued to urge once more, and once more, till a whole
hour had passed away! Conscience again raised her
voice to a note of thunder, and cried: "Ruined youth!
what are you doing?"

It roused me to see my guilt and folly, and I hastened
to the house. I took my Bible and hymn-book and
entered my chamber. Alas! the insulted Spirit had
departed. I tried to weep, but no tears came to my relief.
I tried to recall my morning feelings, but there was no
tenderness in my heart. No one can describe the anguish
of soul I then felt, as I exclaimed: —

"It is too late; the Spirit is grieved away, and I
am lost! Oh, that I had avoided that shop and not
passed by it, but had turned from it and passed away!"

The amusements in which we were engaged were
not sinful in themselves, but they became sinful to me on
account of my peculiar circumstances. I had resolved to
spend the day in retirement, seeking after God. The
Holy Spirit no doubt prompted me to make this resolution, and for me to turn aside to engage in amusements,
however innocent they may have been in themselves, was
now, under these circumstances, trifling with my heavenly Friend, and trifling with the voice of conscience.
And my guilt consisted in my trifling with the Spirit, and
not in the mere fact that I was engaged in recreation.

The Spirit Departed.

EVERY day increased the evidence that I had grieved
away the Spirit of God. The Spirit had indeed departed.

My anxious thoughts by no means ceased at once. For a long time I was a very unhappy youth. Thoughts of what I might have been had I not squandered my time in amusement and trifled with the voice of conscience and the Spirit when they urged me to my chamber, often filled my soul with great bitterness. Yet there was none of that softening and melting of heart that I felt previous to the Spirit's departure. By degrees, however, all these anxious feelings and thoughts wore away and left me almost entirely careless.

Immediately after the conversion of my elder brother and sister, they began to spend a season together, after family worship, on Sabbath evenings, in religious conversation and united prayer. As soon as I began to manifest seriousness, I was invited to accompany them on these seasons to the little chamber. Shall I ever forget those seasons? Shall I ever forget the pleadings of that brother and sister with me, and their intercessions and strong cryings on my behalf? Especially shall I ever forget the earnestness and almost agony with which, after they saw evidence that I was grieving away the Spirit, they urged their entreaties and offered their prayers?

By degrees these seasons became irksome to me; the warnings and expostulations of my brother and sister became unwelcome; and I began to dread the approach of Sabbath evening.

At length, one evening, I contrived to retire to bed so as to prevent an invitation to the little chamber. Oh, how that wounded the hearts of that anxious brother and sister! With what impassioned eloquence and bitter tears did they meet me the next day, and plead with me not to forsake their little meetings. But it was all in vain; I was unmoved. I met with them no more.

I loved my sister. Nothing gave me greater pleasure than to accompany her on a ride or walk. This she understood ; and after I had abandoned the little meetings, and seemed fast relapsing into stupidity, many and many were the ways she devised to make an occasion for a ride or a walk, that she might give vent to the irrepressible yearnings of her heart for my salvation. No one who has not, under similar circumstances, witnessed the gushings forth of strong feelings from a pious sister's heart can appreciate a description of those seasons. Although the anxious entreaties of that sister, one would think, were enough to break and melt a heart of ice, yet my heart had become so hard and so cold that it could resist them all.

Those personal appeals and entreaties became so unwelcome and repulsive that I began to dread and even avoid meeting my sister alone. The strong fraternal love that so recently glowed in my bosom began to grow cold ; yea, more, strange as it may appear, unkindness and even hatred began to take its place! I seemed to repel every effort for my good with the angry words, "Let me alone!"

In such a state was I when the Spirit was departed! I would say to every awakened child or man : "Beware how you trifle with the strivings of the Spirit of God. That Spirit may be grieved away, and all joy and peace, and even natural affection, may depart from your bosom, and you may be left a restless, discontented, and wretched being — a prey to all the vile passions of the soul. Listen, oh, listen now, for your life, to the inviting, melting whispers of that heavenly Spirit."

> " Say, sinner, hath a voice within
> Oft whispered to thy secret soul,
> Urged thee to leave the ways of sin,
> And yield thy heart to God's control?

God's Spirit will not always strive
    With hardened, self-destroying man;
Ye who persist his love to grieve,
    May never hear his voice again.

Sinner, perhaps this very day,
    Thy last accepted time may be;
Oh, shouldst thou grieve him now away,
    Then hope may never smile on thee."

The Spirit Returned.

DURING a part of the winter following I attended a public school in Whitinsville, which is in the town of Northbridge, my birthplace. The school that winter was taught by my elder brother. That neighborhood, the autumn preceding, had been the scene of an extensive revival of religion, and great numbers had been hopefully converted. Many youth, between the ages of nine and fifteen, had shared in this work of grace, and had publicly professed their love for the Saviour. Four of these were brothers and sisters from one family.

Never was there a more delightful scene than the school presented that winter. Religion had diffused its softening, hallowed influence among many of its members. The most entire order and harmony prevailed. When the Scriptures were read, it was as if we heard the voice of the Almighty. Oh, what a solemnity reigned in that little sanctuary, for it seemed like "none other than the house of God and the gate of heaven," when the teacher offered the morning and evening prayer! And what a spectacle did that place often present during the intermission seasons! It was not the scene of loud and boisterous mirth usually witnessed in such places. Oh, no! There was seen a lovely band; and there, in sweetest harmony, were heard their youthful songs of praise and the voice of prayer.

Such were the scenes into which I was introduced. Could I be happy there? How uncongenial to my state of mind was every thing around me — the countenances and conversation of many of my school-mates, yea, and almost the very atmosphere by which I was surrounded. Every thing constantly reminded me of the little chamber and of those little meetings where I often listened to a brother's and a sister's earnest intercessions for my salvation. And for a few weeks I was wretched. I was angry with myself and with every body and every thing around me.

After a few weeks I began, almost unconsciously, to contrast myself — a restless, unhappy, and wretched youth — with my pious school-mates. The calmness, peace of mind, and ineffable happiness, and that tender love for each other which they seemed to possess, I knew were the fruits of their religion. I knew — for I have before said that I enjoyed the instructions of Christian parents — that only by repentance towards God and faith in the Saviour could I be made to feel and enjoy what they felt and enjoyed. I knew, too, that without the influences of the Holy Spirit I could never exercise repentance and faith.

I then recalled those days when the Spirit, in a voice so tender and persuasive, urged me to repent and believe on the Saviour. I remembered how I trifled with that kind voice, and in an evil hour, when, perhaps, my foot was almost on the threshold of salvation, I yielded to the enticing voice of the tempter; and oh, how did the sin of grieving the blessed Spirit, now like a mountain weight, press down my soul into the very dust! The struggle was long and dreadful. At times despair seemed my only portion.

The sympathy and prayers of all the pious youth of the school and of Christians in the neighborhood were enlisted in my behalf. With what earnestness did these young disciples, as they took me by the arm, repeat to me the precious promises of the Bible, and entreat me to cast myself upon the Saviour of the chief of sinners. How often, during the hours of school, did they exhibit the deep anxiety they felt for my salvation, by their kind notes, literally wet with their tears. But all this was in vain. The thought that I had grieved the Spirit seemed to shut out from my mind every ray of hope. I exclaimed: " There can be no salvation for me. I have grieved the Spirit, and he will never, never return ! "

But the Spirit had already returned and was doing his heavenly work. The promise, " Him that cometh to me I will in no wise cast out," broke in upon the cloud of midnight darkness that hung over my mind. I saw that the blood of Christ could wash out the deepest stains of sin.

At length, to the great joy of my pious associates, I was led to hope in the pardoning mercy of God.

Boys' Missionary Society.

AMONG some of my early religious experiences was a feeling of sympathy for the darkened heathen, who had never heard the good news of salvation — had never heard the dear name of Jesus. At that time the work of sending missionaries with the gospel to the heathen world was comparatively new. The American Board of Missions had been formed only a few years, and a missionary society among the young was hardly known. The more I thought about the heathen, the more anxious I felt to do something to aid in this missionary work.

The church where I attended meeting was more than three miles from my home. My young associates were mostly in the neighborhood of the church. Several of them had become interested in religion, and, like myself, had publicly professed their love to the Saviour.

Among my plans to aid in sending the gospel to the heathen, was to form a "Boys' Missionary Society." I talked with my young friends about it. I drew up a sort of constitution, in which it was stated that any boy could become a member by the annual payment of fifty cents.

After getting my plan well-nigh perfected, and getting the approval of a number of boys, I told my father what I wanted to do. The fervent petitions of my father every day at the family altar that the gospel might be sent to the poor heathen had been a great means of awakening and constantly increasing my interest in this subject. Somehow, and most unexpectedly to me, my father did not seem to approve of my plan. He doubted about my giving fifty cents in this way. That was quite a sum for me to promise every year.

I was greatly disappointed. I also felt mortified that I must be the first to fail in carrying out the plan I had myself proposed.

May election — the great holiday, at that time, in Massachusetts — was near at hand. My father was to be absent for several days, but he had told me I might hire a neighbor's horse and spend election with some cousins who lived ten miles distant.

After my father had left home, my mother, who had learned of my disappointment, had one of those ever-to-be-remembered Christian, motherly talks with me. She told me if I was willing to forego my visit to my cousins', I might have the money it would cost to join the Boys' Missionary Society. She knew my father would not object.

This was most joyful news, and I was ready cheerfully to make the sacrifice. My mother also told me I might, if I wished, go into town and spend election with my young friends.

Had not the unexpected arrival, election morning, of several other cousins pleasantly detained me at home, I would have been with a company of fifteen of my young friends in town, who spent a part of the day together. Among other amusements in which this company engaged, they had a row in two boats upon a large pond in the neighborhood. They went upon a beautiful island and had a pleasant picnic. On their return, all joyful and happy in their songs, the boat, containing eight young men and maidens, was suddenly upset, and four interesting misses, two of them sisters, found a watery grave! What a pall of gloom and grief this sad event cast over the whole town! Thousands were present when all four of those lovely forms were laid in the same grave!

With what solemnity and gratitude did I think of the mysterious providence that prevented me that day from being, as I expected to be, with that party, and perhaps being a victim of that melancholy disaster. It led me to a new consecration of myself to the Saviour, and inspired me with new zeal in my missionary interest.

The Boys' Missionary Society was soon after formed with a goodly membership. This society — one of the earlier juvenile missionary associations of the day — continued its good work for several years, till I left my home to fit myself for what has been my life-work in the gospel

ministry.   My interest in missions increased till, for
several years while pursuing my studies, my heart was
set on Africa as the field of my future labors.   But God
in his wisdom assigned me a different but most delightful
field for a life-work among the young in our own land.
And in no phase of this work have I ever felt a deeper
interest — next to that of the conversion of the young —
than in enlisting them early in the cause of Christian
benevolence, in earning and saving the means of helping
to send the good news of salvation throughout the world.

The Dark Closet.

AFTER I became interested in religion, in seeking a
place for retirement for my secret devotions, I thought of
a large closet out of the spare chamber.   That closet
was the place where my mother kept her blankets, com-
forters, and various kinds of bed-clothes.   It was large,
and without a window.   When the door was shut it was
total darkness; no eye but that of Him who "seeth in
secret" could behold any one who there sought retirement from the world.

In that closet I erected my altar for secret prayer.   It
was my Bethel; and none but God can ever know the
Bethel seasons I there enjoyed in communing with the
Saviour in that time of my first love, and until I left
my home to prepare for the work of the gospel ministry.

In one of my visits to my dear old home years after
I had left it, as I was "company," I occupied at night the
spare chamber.   In the morning I had a desire to visit
the dark closet and see how it would seem to shut the
door and pray to my Father which is in secret as I was
wont to do in my young days.   I opened the door, and
what a scene greeted my eyes!   There in the center of

the closet stood a chair, and before that chair there was a cushion in which there were deep prints, where some one, evidently, was accustomed to kneel in secret worship. And who could it be? Who but my own blessed mother, who had prayed all her ten children into the kingdom? What a hallowed spot did it seem to me! A thrill of sacred awe came over me, and a voice almost seemed to say, as it did to Moses at the burning bush: "Put off thy shoes from off thy feet, for the place whereon thou standest is holy ground."

We gaze with interest upon the desk at which a distinguished author composed his works of world-wide fame, at the studio of a great artist, at the chair where sat a renowned statesman or hero; but what are all these to the prints in that cushion, where knelt that dear "mother in Israel" in her communings with the Saviour, and where she "had power with God," as she wrestled with the angel in prayer for her children and for the upbuilding of the Redeemer's kingdom!

CHAPTER VI.

A FEW rods north-east from the village referred to in Chapter III, and near a burial ground, or, as an Irishman put it, "convanient to the grave-yard," with its white grave-stones and long rows of tombs, stood our red district school-house. During the winter months, from seventy-five to one hundred scholars, from the village and the farm-houses for a mile around, thither resorted for instruction. Although the Bible was daily read in school, yet no master ever accompanied it with the voice of prayer, or ever taught his pupils that "the fear of the Lord is the beginning of wisdom."

During the intermission at noon, a large part of the misses who remained, and sometimes of the lads also, were occupied in practicing the lessons they received at an evening school for the education of the feet instead of the head. This kind of education was very popular with some, and they made much better progress in it than they did in the education of their minds. Whether they found it in subsequent life more serviceable to them as farmers, mechanics, housewives, etc., I am not able to say.

In the summer of my seventeenth year I became personally interested in the subject of religion, and made a public profession of that interest by uniting with the church. My older brother and sister and myself were the only young persons in that part of the town who had made such a profession.

Our "joining the church" was a subject of much conversation, wonder, and even ridicule among all classes in
the neighborhood. Much that was very trying to our
feelings we were obliged to hear and witness.

The villagers, old and young, to amuse themselves and
to ridicule religion, invented a story that our parents had
"hired their children to join the church"; and with this
story they would often taunt us. But instead of exciting
our anger, as they wished to do, the influence of such ridicule was to drive us more frequently to our closet, where
we obtained grace to endure it all with a meek, uncom-
plaining, and forgiving spirit. And we often counted it
all joy that we fell into these diverse trials of our faith,
which, I trust, worked in us patience.

The time was now approaching for the commencement
of the public winter school. This was to be my last
season at that school. And no one who has not been
similarly situated can understand the deep and painful
solicitude with which I looked forward to my attendance.

I was probably the first professedly pious youth that
had ever entered that school-house! And there I was to
be brought into close intercourse with nearly one hundred
children and youth, most of whom had been educated to
sneer at religion and every thing serious. What a place
for a Christian youth to stand up alone! I must become
a spectacle to the whole school — a mark at which every
one would aim the arrows of ridicule. All this I foresaw;
and many were my seasons of earnest prayer for strength
equal to my day, and grace that should be sufficient for
me; and also that I might, by my consistent conduct, my
meekness and patience under opposition and ridicule,
constrain some to glorify my heavenly Father. To my
excellent Christian mother, too, I often resorted, to

unbosom my anxieties and to seek her sympathy, coun-
sels, and prayers.

At length the day for the school to commence arrived.
With a mother's blessing and, as I felt, a Saviour's smile,
I went, cast down, yet rejoicing, to the place where I
expected trials awaited me. And my expectations were
indeed realized ; but the Lord was on my side and I was
not moved. At night my heart was full of joy on account
of the grace that enabled me to pray for my opposers :
"Father, forgive them ; for they know not what they
do."

"Father," said Charles Willard, one of my class-mates,
one day just before the commencement of the winter
school — "father, Asa Bullard is going to school this
winter."

"Well, my son, what of it ? "

"Why, you know he has joined the church, and I
mean to do all I can to vex him."

"Oh, no, Charles ! I would n't go to troubling him, if
he lets you alone," replied Mr. Willard, who, though not
then a professor, was a respecter of religion.

"Well," said Charles, "I mean to watch him, and he 's
got to walk pretty straight, or I shall appear against him."

In all this Charles was as good as his word. Many
were his endeavors, by unkind words, actions, and looks, to
tease and, if possible, to irritate his class-mate. Nothing
would have delighted him more than to see me out of
temper.

"There !" he would have tauntingly said, "there 's
your Christian, getting angry ! "

He well understood, as the ungodly generally do, just
how Christians ought to act. He knew that the indulgence of such a temper, even under ridicule and unpro-

voked insult, is inconsistent with the meek, forgiving spirit of the gospel.

At one time Charles would send me a note, in school time, addressing me as " parson " or " deacon," or in some way deriding me about my " religion." At another time, by means of some grimace or gesture, or ludicrous draw-ing, he would excite among the scholars near him a smile of derision at my expense. All this, however, I seemed to have grace to bear with a Christian temper. When reviled, like my divine Master, I " reviled not again," but bore it meekly. Now and then a tear of grief and pity would appear in my eyes, but no flush of passion was seen upon my cheek.

Supposing there was no hope of doing my school-mates any spiritual good by direct efforts till I had in a measure softened their prejudices by the influence of a silent example, I carefully avoided all intercourse with them. I never mingled with them at recess or intermission, so that they seldom had the opportunity, except for a few moments as the school closed at noon and at night, openly to assail me with their ridicule.

One day, in a neighborhood about a mile from the village, there was held an afternoon and evening religious meeting. Among the attendants was a young cousin of Charles Willard, who was brought up with him as a sister. During the recess I had a conversation with her on the subject of religion, and found that she was anxious about her salvation.

" I wish," she said, as we were about to close our interview, " I wish you would talk with Cousin Charles."

"Talk with Charles!" I said to myself. " Oh, how he would scoff and deride ! It would be casting pearls before swine !" And I then informed her of the manner in which her cousin had been treating me. She was greatly surprised and grieved to hear this, but said : —

"Well, I think he has for a few days seemed to be serious, and I wish you would converse with him."

How my heart throbbed with joy at the very thought that such a thing could be true! In reflecting a moment I remembered that the conduct of Charles towards me had, for several days, been changed. He had made no attempts to ridicule or in any way to molest me.

"I now recollect," I said, "that several times of late Charles has seemed to be trying to get near me; but, supposing it was for no good purpose, I have avoided him. Charles Willard serious!" I exclaimed with emotion. "Oh, I hope it is so! I will surely seek an interview with him at the earliest opportunity."

What a subject was this for me that night to carry to my closet! Earnest were my petitions that God would give me *one* friend in school who would sympathize and rejoice with me in all I was called to suffer for Christ and his cause.

The next morning I sought divine guidance, and anew commended my class-mates to the mercy of God. During the forenoon session Charles appeared sedate and thoughtful. With deep and anxious emotions did I observe him, and many were the silent prayers I offered in his behalf. Several times I caught his eye and exchanged kind looks; and these looks, so unlike those of the scorn and contempt that I had been accustomed to receive, went to my very heart. Already I had forgiven all his unkindness and I longed to meet him as a friend.

As the school closed at noon Charles immediately began to make his way among the scholars towards the one he had so often and unkindly injured. Unobserved by others, we met and took each other cordially by the hand.

"Charles," I asked affectionately, "would n't you like to take a walk?" And together we left the noisy, thoughtless throng, and directed our way to the calm, quiet retreat of a beautiful grove near by. For a few moments we walked on in silence. At length, encouraged by the whole appearance of my friend, I broke the silence by the inquiry: —

"Charles, I want to ask how you feel in regard to the subject of religion?"

The inquiry was answered by a burst of emotion and a flood of tears! We entered the grove and seated ourselves under a large oak, and there, leaning upon each other, we wept together. After our emotions became a little calmed, Charles made a full and most heart-felt disclosure of his feelings. He mentioned his conversation with his father before the school commenced, and confessed all the unkind efforts he had been making to tease and vex his friend; and he earnestly sought forgiveness. This was most cheerfully granted, and again our emotions found relief in tears.

"For some time," said Charles, "I have been very unhappy, although I have continued my opposition to you. O Asa, the patience and meekness with which you have received all my unkind treatment often touched my heart, and sometimes almost caused me to sink. Many a time have I longed to feel as you seemed to feel, and to enjoy the peace of mind and happiness that you appeared to enjoy. Oh, pray for me, that I may be forgiven and be happy with you."

After a full and free interchange of feelings, together we knelt under that majestic oak, and I poured out my soul in tears and strong cryings in behalf of my once thoughtless and ridiculing, but now broken-hearted, class-mate.

For several days Charles was borne down under very deep convictions of sin, and I was as deeply burdened with anxiety on his account. I knew by the most painful personal experience that the Holy Spirit, now so evidently striving with my friend, might be easily grieved away, and my friend be left to renew, with sevenfold violence, all his opposition and ridicule.

We often repaired together to the grove, there to converse on heavenly themes and seek for pardoning mercy. With all the solicitude that pious parents feel for an anxious child, did I labor to point out the way of eternal life, and exhort and entreat my friend to believe on the Lord Jesus Christ that he might be saved. Many were the letters, full of exhortation and warning, all breathing the most heart-felt interest and lively concern for his spiritual welfare, that I daily wrote him.

At length, while seeking God in our favorite resort in the grove, prayer was heard, and light and peace broke in upon the mind of Charles, and joy and gladness filled my heart. The new song of praise for pardoning love was put into the lips of the one, and of thanksgiving for the gift of a companion of his joys and sorrows, into those of the other. My raptures were not unlike those of the lone traveler, when, "a stranger in a strange land," surrounded by those whose language he knows not and with whom he feels connected by no tie of interest or sympathy, he suddenly meets one from his native country, with interests, sympathies, and associations common with himself. Who that has not been a solitary Christian youth in such a school, and seen, in connection with his own labors, a class-mate converted from a persecuting Saul into a meek and praying Paul, can rightly estimate the happiness and joy that I now experienced? Strong and endearing, and daily increasing, was the brotherly attachment that now existed between us. Our friendship was like that of David and Jonathan.

George Smith, another of my class-mates, had participated with Charles in much of his opposition to me. He had marked Charles' change of conduct. He often narrowly observed him when the cloud of sorrow was on his countenance and the burden of sin was upon his soul. He saw the change when the cloud passed away and the sunshine of peace and joy appeared. He gazed and admired, while in his heart he hated the change. He witnessed the growing attachment between his two class-mates and their apparent happiness.

Charles, only a little while before wondering how I could so patiently and meekly bear all his ridicule, was now bearing ridicule with the same meekness and patience himself. This was indeed marvelous to George. The more he thought of it, and the more he observed the conduct of us two friends, the more his wonder increased. All was a perfect mystery.

"There must be something," no doubt he often thought within himself, "in this religion to which I am a stranger."

As he pondered this subject he wished he understood more about it and about the secret of our apparent enjoyment. The Spirit of God, though he knew it not, was awakening in his mind these thoughts and desires and leading him by a way he knew not. A slight shade of thoughtfulness and anxiety began to appear in his countenance. This was quickly seen by me and communicated to my new friend; and it became a matter of anxious joy, consultation, and prayer. Erelong these three classmates were on their way to that Bethel-spot in the beautiful grove. For awhile pride and shame prevented George from acknowledging any special interest in the subject of religion; but at length the sigh and the unbidden tear revealed what in words he was unwilling to admit.

For several days we continued to spend a season together in the grove. Every possible effort was made to lead George to the Saviour. His convictions became deep and his distress almost overpowering. Never will his two friends forget how his agonizing inquiry, "What shall I do? Oh, what *shall* I do?" went to their hearts, and with what importunity they pleaded with God in his behalf.

His anxiety continued from day to day unabated. He seemed to feel that he was a lost and ruined sinner; but with all the instructions we could give him, our explanations of the way to the Saviour, of repentance and faith, and all our earnest exhortations and prayers, there he remained. Our efforts in his behalf and our sympathy for him he tenderly felt and always met with many testimonies of gratitude.

During the exercises of school one forenoon, George was seen very deeply engrossed with a book. This was soon observed by his two anxious friends. Alive as we were to his dearest interest, we watched every change in his appearance with the solicitude that an anxious mother watches the changing symptoms of a sick child.

The perusal of that book was evidently producing a disastrous effect on the mind of George. That deep, settled anxiety that had appeared in his countenance for several days was giving place to a sort of uneasy recklessness and desperation of feeling.

What could be the character of the book that was working such a change in his appearance and evidently in his feeling? We soon ascertained that it was a work on that system of error that says, in the language of the old serpent to our first parents, "Thou shalt not surely die." The great deceiver has no mightier instrument of quieting a troubled conscience, hushing the secret whisperings of the Spirit, and lulling the soul into the slumbers of the second death! Our anxiety for his spiritual welfare was now brought almost into agony. Had George, as we were gazing upon him, been suddenly smitten down, a lifeless corpse, our alarm and distress could scarcely have been greater. In every possible way — by the unutterable anxiety of our countenances and by our notes, in which we expostulated, warned, and entreated — we besought him to desist from this deliberate act of self-ruin to his soul; but all was in vain. He persisted, thus deliberately closing his ears to the entreaties of his friends and the warnings of conscience.

From this sad day all seriousness disappeared, and he could even jest at his former feelings and the prayers and entreaties of his anxious class-mates. The Spirit was grieved away, and the voice of conscience hushed into a slumber so deep, so death-like, that there is reason to fear nothing but the trump of the last great day will ever awake it.

But on whom rested the fearful responsibility of having placed that conscience-silencing, Spirit-grieving, and soul-ruining volume in the hands of that once anxious but now hardened youth? Alas! it was a professed friend and class-mate, Daniel Thompson, who approached him as Joab did Amasa, with a kiss on his lips but a sword in his hand. It is true that friend was then, like all his

class-mates, but a youth, and he was only acting out the
principles in which his parents had educated him. But
all this can be no excuse for a deliberate attempt to stop
a fellow-mortal in his inquiries after the way of life, and
turn him back into the beaten pathway to perdition.

And now a few words in regard to the subsequent history of these class-mates.

Charles, after having pursued a course of preparatory
studies for a few years, entered the ministry, and is in
New England, laboring with a good degree of success in
the vineyard of the Lord. We have not often met, but
have ever been warm friends, both cherishing the most
tender recollection of our last winter at the public school
and the solemn and interesting scenes connected with
that dear old sacred oak in the beautiful grove.

Daniel is, so far as I know, an industrious and respectable
citizen. But he still adheres to that system of error by
which he was the unhappy instrument of engulfing in
ruin all the immortal hopes and interests of his classmate
George.

But alas for poor George, the once anxious inquirer after
the way of life and salvation! What must be said of
him? So sad and mournful was his short life of intemperance and opposition to every thing sacred that I can
not dwell upon it. But let all my young readers learn
a lesson from it, and make use of opportunities while they
are theirs.

CHAPTER VII.

ATTENDING ACADEMY. — MY FIRST SCHOOL. — DECIDING TO
PREPARE FOR THE MINISTRY.

IN the spring of 1821 my oldest brother and sister and myself attended, one term, the academy at Uxbridge. This was my first experience of leaving my home. But as my brother and sister were with me, there was no especial loneliness experienced. Every Sabbath evening we had a season of religious conversation and prayer at my sister's room. Some pleasant new acquaintances were formed among the students, and the term was, in all respects, one of interest and profit.

In the autumn of 1822 I attended the academy in Monson one term. There was nothing of marked interest during that period — my first absence from home alone — except that I had a severe attack of what physicians call nostalgia, but in common language is called home-sickness. This disease is so well known that it need not be described.

In the winter of that year, when I was a little more than eighteen years of age, I taught school in the east part of Sutton, in what was called the Hatherway district. One event in connection with my teaching there may be worthy of notice.

For two or three winters there had been some insubordination in the school. Soon after it commenced that winter, word came to me that Charles ——, my oldest scholar, had given out word that he intended to put the young teacher out of the school-house.

For several days it was evident that he was preparing for a conflict. Just before closing school one afternoon, as I passed near him, I quietly and unobserved by any one requested him to stop a few moments after school.

When we were alone, I informed him in as pleasant a manner as possible of what I had heard. I then assured him that there would be no opportunity for any such conflict between him and his teacher. He was then informed of the business for which the school committee had hired me — to teach, and not to see who was the stronger, some one of the scholars or the teacher. He was told what a large proportion of the taxes paid by the parents in that district was for school purposes ; and that the parents had a right to expect that I should be as faithful in teaching their children as any one would be in performing any work for which he was hired.

" Now, Charles," said I, " I shall have no time to turn away from my work of teaching to test my strength with any of my older scholars, who know better than to interrupt the peace and prosperity of the school. I shall just request the committee to remove any such disturbers of our work from the school. I should be very sorry to have any of my older scholars — and especially my oldest and best one — taken out of school. You are almost as old as your teacher. With a diligent use of your time, in one or two winters you yourself will be as well qualified to teach as he is. And I want to do all I can this winter to aid you, and also all the scholars, in making such progress in the business for which the school is kept that at the close it shall be said by the committee and all the parents that this has been the best school they have ever had. I want this should be the case, both for my own sake and also for the sake of all the scholars. Our success as teacher and scholars will be judged of by the orderly character of the school and by the progress that is made in the various branches of study by the scholars. Now, Charles, all this will depend a good deal on the older scholars. If they are studious and orderly, and show an interest in the peace and improvement of the school, the younger ones will be likely to do the same. So I want you, my oldest scholar, to take the lead and be my assistant in this matter."

I then approached him, and extending my hand, said: "May I depend on you, Charles, to do this?"

The tears came in his eyes as he took my hand and pledged his help. He walked quite a distance towards my boarding-place, away from his home, while we had a very pleasant talk.

It hardly need be said that Charles fulfilled his promise and was a most studious and well-behaved scholar all through the winter, and a great help to the teacher.

Was not this a much better way than to have had a conflict before the school?

In the spring of this year I began to consider the subject whether I ought not to prepare myself to preach the gospel. As it was quite a trial for my father to give up his plans to entrust more fully the management of the farm to my older brother, and accede to that brother's wishes to obtain an education, I resolved not to mention my desires to my father. Instead of this, I arranged with my oldest sister to be my mediator in the matter. After stating freely to her my longing to fit myself for that important profession, I left it with her to confer with both mother and father on the subject. Sister entered heartily into my plans. She had frequent conversations on the subject with our mother, who approved of my purposes.

At length the matter was laid before father. This was while I was absent with my school, and while at home, at one time, father informed me of what he had learned in regard to my wishes, from my sister and also from mother. He then said that such a step was a very important one. It would be a course that would involve large expense; and the thought of preparing for that sacred office was a very solemn one. He then said he wanted me carefully to consider the subject and let him know what I thought it best for me to do. I told him " I had thought the subject over with a great deal of seriousness and prayer; and I had already made up my mind to prepare for college as soon as I became of age. I did not wish to do any thing that would increase his care and anxiety so long as he rightly claimed my help."

A few hours after this pleasant and perfectly free conversation, he met me again and kindly said : " You had better go back to your school, and at its close go with your brother, who has entered Amherst College, to Amherst Academy and commence your studies."

It was pleasant to see how much easier my good father found it, when he had once made the sacrifice of giving up one son, to give up the second ; and I believe it became easier and easier till five of his boys started for college.

We children felt, with our parents, that so far as possible we should share alike in regard to pecuniary favors. When we, one after another, became of age, a few hundred dollars were given us. Those of us who left home for study before we became of age were charged for our time just what it would cost to secure men to take our places. Then all the expenses of our education were readily met by our father, and we gave our notes on interest for the same, to be paid as we could obtain the means after we entered upon our work.

This plan we all approved, and it made us economical in our expenses, and taught us important lessons, in many respects, that were of great value to us in after life. We knew that the whole family at home, father and mother, brothers and sisters, were economizing in many ways on our account, to furnish the means we needed to pursue our studies.

In my own case it was many years after I entered my profession before my indebtedness for my education was canceled. When in college it was often a wonder to me, how the sons of parents in moderate circumstances — sons of clergymen, in some cases, with small income, and when they knew every member of the family at home was making the greatest sacrifices in their behalf — could be so thoughtless and prodigal. If every term students were obliged to sign a note for the money they expend, it might check their prodigality.

CHAPTER VIII.

PREPARATORY AND COLLEGE COURSE.

IN the spring of 1822 I entered Amherst Academy, where I spent about one year and seven months. My class-mate, Thomas Boutelle, agreed to be my room-mate when we entered college. But near the close of our preparatory course he concluded to spend another year in the academy, as it would have been wise for me also to have done.

By his decision I was left without a room-mate for college, and I threatened a suit for breach of promise unless he would provide a substitute, and one as congenial as himself. He recommended his cousin, Asaph Boutelle, then in the academy at New Ipswich, N. H.

I opened a correspondence with him, which resulted in a mutual agreement, though we had never met, to enter this interesting relation of room-mates. And we were so well satisfied with the union that we continued it for three years; and we should have continued it through the whole course, had not circumstances prevented. We were in perfect sympathy in our tastes and in our religious sentiments and feelings, and in regard to the work of life for which we were studying. No two class-mates were more attached to each other than we; and this attachment continued till my dear friend finished his course in the ministry and received his reward.

I entered college in 1824, when I was twenty years of age. The college was then in its infancy, and it had a hard struggle for existence. The students, scarcely less than the trustees and faculty, were greatly interested in all that was done to secure its endowment and its charter, and great was the enthusiasm when the act of incorporation was obtained.

Rev. Heman Humphrey, D.D., was our president at that time, and our professors were Messrs. Edward Hitchcock, Nathan W. Fiske, Solomon Peek, Samuel M. Worcester, and Jacob Abbott. Ebenezer S. Snell was then tutor.

In consequence of my home training, as described in Chapter IV, the laws and rules of college never came in conflict with my wishes. I never felt inclined to join any college strikes. Sometimes I was a little troubled lest some of those inclined to lawlessness would think I was green or wanting in courage. But I could really find nothing I wanted to do in violation of the requirement of college, or that would bring me into conflict with the officers whose business it was to look after the unruly. It was no virtue in me, but it was the result of my early training.

There was one thing, perhaps, that helped to keep me watchful over my conduct in college. The year before I went to Amherst for study, two students of college from Sutton were sent home for insubordination. It seemed to me at the time that it must be a terrible disgrace to themselves and a most grievous mortification to their parents and friends. I said to myself: "What a dreadful thing it would be should my brother, who was then in college, be thus disgraced!" And so, in the simplicity of my heart, I wrote him a long letter, beseeching him to be careful and do nothing that would bring such a disgrace upon him and such grief upon his home. And this I did, although that brother was a professing Christian and was studying for the ministry! Still, the bare thought that such a thing could happen was to me most appalling. This made such an impression upon me that it no doubt served to make me more watchful over my own conduct while in college.

While in the academy I became very much interested in the religious meetings, both in the academy and in the village. Rev. Daniel A. Clark was then the pastor of the Congregational church near the college. I often was with him in the meetings among his people.

During a time of unusual religious interest in the academy, President Humphrey preached one evening. He spoke without notes. I felt much alarmed as he mentioned his text, which indicated that he was going to speak on the doctrine of election. That subject was more frequently presented in those days than it is now. I feared the preaching on that subject would check the revival. But what was my surprise to learn that three young persons, under the influence of that same sermon and while they were listening to it, were led to hope in the electing love and mercy of God! And ever since then I have felt that there is no doctrine or truth in the Word of God, if properly and in a scriptural way presented, that will be out of place in a revival. God's truth will not grieve away the Holy Spirit.

Very early in my studies at Amherst, my attention was directed to the colored people in town, of whom there were quite a number. In the family where for awhile I boarded, there was a colored servant whom we all called "Mother Phillis." She was a widow about sixty years of age. She was an intelligent and devoted Christian. Very often I used to get up early Monday mornings, when she was engaged in washing, that I might have a good religious talk with her. Those seasons were more inspiring to my religious feelings than many a sermon.

This interest in Mother Phillis made me acquainted with her children and their families. And early in college I formed a Bible class in a private dwelling, about a mile distant. This class was kept up till I left college. It was one of the most interesting classes I ever taught. We usually had a room full of persons of all ages.

My interest in this class of people was such that for two or three years my heart was very much set upon spending my life in Africa. Mother Phillis was most deeply interested in this class. After I left Amherst, in answer to a letter she thus expresses the overflowings of a grateful, pious soul : —

I improve this opportunity to answer your kind letter. The past acquaintance of which you speak is ever to be remembered by me: for our sweet conversation about God I can not forget. When I call to remembrance those past hours in which I took so much delight in talking about God and his love to man, holy joy warms my aged heart. Even now it is filled with sacred love and thanksgiving to God that he gave me a friend with whom I could converse so freely upon the soul-reviving subject of redeeming love.

I carried your letter to the class and it was read. They were all rejoiced to hear from you, and to know that you had not forgotten them. Oh, that I had the happy news to tell you that the class, or even one of them, had begun to rejoice in hope of salvation through a crucified Redeemer! But alas! it is not so. But be not discouraged. We know not what the Lord in his great mercy may do for their precious souls. Still continue your prayers in faith for us, knowing that the prayer of faith availeth much.

Our little class is becoming more interesting, and we have begun to get a library. May God revive his work in this class until all shall go forth joyfully praising God and the Lamb!

I thank you for your kind exhortations. May God strengthen me by his almighty grace to do my duty better, and live nearer to him than I have hitherto done; and may he crown all your undertakings with success!

In 1829, while I was at Andover Theological Seminary, she wrote to a mutual friend of ours a most touching letter, expressing the greatest sorrow and disappointment that her old friend and teacher was not to be at the commencement at Amherst as was expected.

"Why did we indulge the hope," she writes, "of seeing you and our former teacher here this fall? Our fondest expectations are now cut off forever. Tell Mr. B. that all our class have cherished the strongest hopes of seeing him. Even little Harriet says : 'Grandma, Mr. Bullard is coming next week!' But alas! her expectations failed with ours.

"A few weeks since I said : 'Commencement is close by, and then I shall see my best friend ; yes, my eyes, ere they are closed in death, shall see him once more.' But now I know that my eyes shall see him no more, and my ears, which have so oft heard the voice of prayer from his lips, shall hear his voice no more. Tell Mr. B. that our Bible class has improved some, and our teachers very much."

Is it strange that such appreciation of the little service I was able to give this class led me to feel a very deep interest in them and in behalf of this race every-where?

During most of my vacations in college I taught school ; one winter in South Weymouth. The school-house was very small for the large number of scholars. There was a large, old-fashioned fire-place, but the house was heated by a stove, sometimes literally heated. The spacious fire-place was utilized by placing in it several seats, which were occupied by some of the smaller children. Then boards were placed across the passage-ways between the tiers of seats so as to accommodate several more of the scholars.

The people in Weymouth were in the habit of making a good deal of the closing examinations of their schools. I was informed that many of the older scholars in my school — as the examination was the last session of the school — were in the habit of absenting themselves. So I told the school, a few weeks before the close, that there ought to be a new and larger school-house in this district. This house was quite too strait, too small, for such a large number of scholars, and that it was old and every way inconvenient. And then I told them "I would almost promise them a new school-house before the next winter if they would do one thing. Let every scholar be present at the examination. Fill every seat so that all the parents and friends who come to the examination will have to stand, and so that they can see how inconvenient the house is for so many scholars, and I believe the district will at once build a new and more spacious house."

The examination day came, and every scholar was present and every seat was occupied. The friends came in and filled every inch of space — the floor — between the seats and the entry, and numbers were on the outside looking in at the windows. The crowd was such that the scholars, when they recited, had to stand upon their seats to be seen! It is enough to say that the people of "Fore-Street District" saw and felt the necessity of a larger and and a better school-house for their children ; and the next season it was provided, and the teacher's promise was fulfilled, much to the joy and comfort of the scholars. Of course this event made the teacher a very popular man among the scholars.

Two winters I taught the district school in what is called "Eight Lots," in the town of Sutton, about two miles from my old home. Then one winter I taught the grammar school in the town of Canton, Conn. And I find, among my old papers and documents, two written addresses that I delivered to my school, one near the beginning and the other at the close. Judging from these addresses, and from my recollections, religious instruction was made quite prominent ; and teacher and scholars were on the most friendly terms, so that the separation, at the close, was very tender ; and all carried away pleasant memories of the few weeks we had spent together.

Shortly after Amherst College received its charter in 1825, measures were taken to form a college church, and in March, 1826, one was formed under the name of "The Church of Christ in Amherst College."

The college was founded by the prayers and toils and sacrifices of Christian men, and it has ever been, in a remarkable sense, a Christian college. It has often been the scene of the special out-pouring of the Holy Spirit. There were two revivals of remarkable interest during my connection with college, in 1827 and 1828.

In Professor Tyler's "History of Amherst College during its First Half-century," he has used the following extract of a letter, which, by his request, I wrote him, in regard to an incident in the latter revival : —

Only a few weeks before the close of the term President Humphrey was all ready one Saturday to start for his former home in Pittsfield, when some students called on him and told him that there were signs of seriousness in college. Dr. Humphrey turned out his horse and gave up his visit. At evening prayers he stopped the pious students and gave them a most solemn exhortation to earnest prayer and faithful labor for a revival. The Holy Spirit was evidently present. Sabbath day several were hopefully converted, and for a day or two conversions were constantly occurring, when all at once the work seemed to stop.

Monday evening the president again stopped the pious students after prayers and, in the most solemn and anxious manner, said: "Something is wrong!"

Never shall I forget that day! and many will probably remember while they live that judgment-like Monday. The students were gathered every-where in little clusters, as solemn as if some great calamity had just fallen upon us. Soon the college was one great house of prayer. In every entry and from many a room could be heard the voice of the most earnest, agonizing supplications. From that hour the work went on. Those who were bowed down under conviction of sin found relief, and there were conversions almost every day till the close of the term.

In these revivals there were many most remarkable cases of conversion ; some of them of those who were, as many felt, the most hopeless, as they were certainly the most reckless, in college. Among the converts were the late Rev. A. W. McClure, D.D., the eloquent and able preacher, author, editor, etc. ; and Henry Lyman, the devoted missionary, who fell a martyr among the Battas of Sumatra.

There were many events of interest, serious and comical, that might be mentioned, connected with my four years in college. It may not be out of place to record the following incident : —

A few years ago I was at the commencement services at my Alma Mater. At the prize speaking, with two other gentlemen, I was requested to sit on the platform with the professor who presided. At the close of the evening session, as the professor was about to announce the prizes, he said : —

"It may be interesting to the audience to be informed that there is a gentleman on the platform who, sixty years ago, at the first prize speaking in Amherst College, when he was a freshman, spoke and received a prize!"

This singular and most unexpected announcement was received with a burst of applause from the audience. How little we know in regard to our future! We may propose, but God disposes.

Some one, a few days before my class graduated, asked : "What are you going to do after you graduate ?"

My instant reply was: "I am going immediately to Andover Theological Seminary, and right through the course into my work. You don't find me going off to teach, as some of the class are going to do."

A few days after, Prof. Jacob Abbott, my professor in mathematics, sent for me to call at his room. On meeting him he said he had received a letter from Augusta, Me., asking him to send some one to teach a private school of twenty or twenty-five boys, who were fitting for college. He then said he had sent for me, to ask if I would go and take charge of that school.

What a change in all my plans and possibly in my whole life-work that question wrought! In the first place, the asking of that question of me I could not but regard as complimentary to myself. Then, the place and the character of the school seemed very desirable, and so I yielded my proposed plans and followed what seemed to be the leading of providence, and accepted the offer. And it is pleasant, at this distance of time, to be able to say that I never saw occasion to regret the course I then decided to take.

It was always a matter of interest to me to notice how differently some officers in college were regarded by different classes. With one class a professor would be very popular, and perhaps with the next class that came under his instruction, extremely unpopular. I would often inquire with myself: "What is the cause of this difference? Is it likely that the professor is constantly changing? Is he affable with one class and then arbitrary and censorious with the next, or is the change in the temperament and character of the class?"

The following reminiscences of Prof. Jacob Abbott I wrote for the "memorial edition of his Young Christian," prepared by his sons: —

Jacob Abbott was my professor in mathematics and natural philosophy in Amherst College from 1825 to my graduation in 1828. My recollections of him as a professor and as a Christian man have been very pleasant. There was no officer in college who was more uniformly popular and more generally respected by all classes of students than he. He was remarkably paternal, or rather fraternal, in his intercourse with the students. He was always approachable by every one. No one felt repelled from him by his looks and general manners, but rather encouraged to go to him more freely for counsel.

While in perfect accord with all the faculty, in regard to the importance of a healthy college discipline, and ever ready to rebuke wrong-doing, yet there was no air of the autocrat about him, nothing overbearing and dictatorial. There was no officer in college to whom a student in any trouble would sooner go than to him. He knew he would be received kindly, and that the professor would be most ready to give him all the help he was able. There was no one in whose judgment and decision, in regard to any matter between the students, all would more fully confide. I recall one very remarkable case.

A small number of one of the literary societies became disaffected in regard to some action of the society, withdrew and formed a new organization. The seceders claimed a portion of the library. The contest over the matter became very sharp. At length both parties agreed to submit the question to Professor Abbott and abide by his decision. The two parties met, and it was marvelous to see how wisely, impartially, and convincingly he laid the whole subject before the contestants. As he proceeded from one step to another he carried the conscience of every one till, with consummate skill, he brought the parties to his decision. While the decision was very trying to the large majority, they accepted it without a reflection on the judge. No other officer in college, I think, could have arbitrated the case so wisely and secured such ready acceptance of his decision.

As a teacher Mr. Abbott was always popular with the class. He had a remarkable faculty of making the dry study of mathematics attractive. He seemed to have an inexhaustible fund of anecdote and illustration, which he used as felicitously in teaching science as he did subsequently in preparing popular literature for the young. He had a tact in enlisting the interested attention of the class. He threw so much personal interest and enthusiasm into his manner of instructing that he excited a corresponding enthusiasm in the students.

I think very few students were much inclined to deceive him in regard to their lessons or their general conduct, or to play tricks upon him, as some were in the case of some other officials. His dignified and courteous bearing and his affable treatment of all seemed to command the respect of all, and to disarm even those naturally inclined to exhibitions of fun and mischief.

Mr. Abbott was always respected and revered as a truly Christian man. All believed him sincere in what he said and did as a professed follower of Jesus. He entered with great earnestness into all plans and efforts to promote the religious awakenings that frequently existed while he was in college. Many students, now actively engaged in Christian work, or who are, through faith and patience, inheriting the promises, no doubt remember his earnest words of exhortation, counsel, and prayers in connection with their awakenings and early religious experience.

CHAPTER IX.

A YEAR IN AUGUSTA, MAINE.

SOON after graduating, in 1828, I went directly to Augusta, Maine. My journey was in a packet. This was my first experience upon the ocean. It was a wearisome voyage, as we were for a long time becalmed. The rolling of the vessel, as we lay in the hot sun, was any thing but pleasant to the few half-seasick passengers. I had just enough of nausea to prevent me from patronizing the steward for nearly two days. I suffered more than I did in my voyages to and from Glasgow in 1880, for I was not at all uncomfortable in those trips, though our return one was extremely rough.

As we entered the Kennebec River and our discomfort left us, the mate brought me a cup of coffee, a nice piece of smoked herring, or " Kennebec turkey," as it is called in Maine, and some sea-crackers. Did ever a king relish the most sumptuous dinner as I did that simple repast ?

My home for the year spent in Augusta was in the most delightful family of the late Rev. Benjamin Tappan, D.D., pastor of the Congregational church in the town. And to make every thing as favorable to me, pecuniarily, as possible, he proposed that I should teach two of his daughters, Elizabeth, now the wife of Rev. E. B. Webb, D.D., late pastor of the Shawmut Church in Boston, and Jane, in Latin, one hour a day out of school, for my board. This proposal was most gladly accepted.

As for the school, which I was told was to consist of twenty or twenty-five boys fitting for college, I did not find, in two respects, what I anticipated. First, the places in which it was held, for we were obliged to make several changes, were any thing but convenient and inviting. And in the next place I found that about every branch of study, from Homer's Iliad to the elementary reader, was to be taught ; and that there must be about as many classes as there were scholars. Of course it was evident, from the first, that no teacher, under such circumstances, could do any justice either to himself or to his pupils. It also greatly increased the labors of the teacher to have so many classes.

With these exceptions the school was found to be very pleasant. The scholars were from the leading families of the town. It was not many weeks before the request came that a class of six or eight young misses might be admitted to the school ; and erelong the number of pupils was thirty-six. This addition to the number at first proposed I consented to, though the teacher's salary was not correspondingly increased.

Yet under all these unfavorable circumstances, so far as any expressions were known, the school was regarded a success. Several of the scholars obtained a liberal education and prepared themselves for the different public professions — four or five of them for the ministry. Rev. Benjamin Tappan, Jr., who read most of Homer's Iliad during the year, was, for several years, pastor of the Winthrop Church, Charlestown, and afterward, for many years, pastor of the Congregational church in Norridgewock, Maine. His wife, Delia Emmons, a daughter of Judge Emmons, of Augusta, and granddaughter of the distinguished divine, Rev. Dr. Emmons, of Franklin, Mass., was also a member of my school.

This year in Augusta was a very busy and, to me, interesting one, outside of the school and the one hour a day in teaching Latin. Soon after commencing the school, by the request of Rev. Dr. Tappan, the pastor, I prepared and read to his people, at the close of the morning sermon, an address on the subject of Sabbath-schools. In a short time I took measures to gather a Bible class on Sabbath afternoons, for colored people. There were only six or eight of that class of persons in the place, but so much interest was awakened that they came from Hallowell, two miles, and even from Gardiner, six miles, and I soon had a class of twenty-five or thirty. I wrote to a friend the following account of this class, which may interest my readers : —

After the exercises of the first Sabbath, I sat down in rather a melancholy mood, and began to think of my Sabbaths spent in Massachusetts. On no public exercise of the Sabbath did my mind rest with such intense interest as my Bible class for the colored people. The realization that the many pleasant seasons spent in that class were now at an end not a little increased my sadness. But the inquiry soon arose in my mind, May there not be some of that neglected people in this place? If so, can they not be collected into a class? On learning that there were two or three small families, consisting, in all, of some six or eight souls, I resolved to search them out. Accordingly, the next Sabbath afternoon I called at one of their dwellings and found a very intelligent-looking woman, who listened with much apparent interest to the explanation of my object, and said that she could not read any, but she should like to learn, so that she might read her Bible. This readiness to enter into my plans greatly encouraged me to hope that a class could be collected with but little difficulty.

As I approached the next dwelling, near by, I heard the loud laugh and the voice of merriment. This damped my early hopes. I stopped, turned about, and well-nigh resolved to abandon my object, at least for that time. But a moment's reflection influenced me to seize the present opportunity and go forward. I entered with some reluctance, and there found six or eight colored persons, some from other towns, who had collected together to spend their Sabbath evening in amusement.

It would be rather difficult for a person not familiar with such scenes to conceive the variety of emotions which the presence of a stranger, especially on such an errand, produced among them. At first they manifested an astonishment bordering on consternation. But as the object of my visit was explained, and the advantages of spending a part of the Sabbath in the study of the Bible mentioned, together with the interest manifested by a class of colored persons in Massachusetts, the first excitement subsided, and some began to show great interest; some appeared indifferent; and some half-concealed a smile of derision.

After some more conversation, they concluded to consider the subject, and decide in reference to it at my next call. During the week I called again, and found my compensation the only thing concerning which they had any further inquiries to make. Being informed that the only compensation expected or wished for was their attendance and improvement, they readily accepted my proposals and appointed the next Sabbath for organization.

On the next Sabbath I found some six or seven assembled, awaiting my arrival. Having implored the aid of the Spirit, without which all our efforts are inefficient, they were requested to read a chapter in the Bible. Some could read with considerable ease, some very little, and some not at all.

I felt that the success of this experiment depended, in a great measure, upon the impression made at the first meeting; and it was so ordered that the impression was most favorable. A very lively interest was evidently awakened among several of the class, who soon visited many of the colored people living two, and even six, miles distant, and told them all about their class and invited their attendance.

On the following Sabbath our number was somewhat enlarged, and the interest increased. One middle-aged female, who barely knew her alphabet, had purchased a Testament, and began to spell out some of the small words. She continued to improve every week, and was soon able to read with the class with some ease. Not unfrequently she would repeat five or ten verses of Scripture which she had learned, with much painstaking, during the week.

One girl, eighteen or twenty years of age, who was quite intelligent, has been of great service in hearing some of the children read and recite their lessons. She usually has recited herself from fifteen to fifty verses every Sabbath. Another little girl of nine recited ten, sometimes forty, verses with great propriety.

Almost every week has shown some increase of interest, sometimes of numbers. During the latter part of autumn the class varied in number from twelve to twenty, some of whom came a distance of six miles, most of them with their new Bibles or Testaments.

About this time one of the class suggested the expediency of meeting a part of the time at an adjoining town, for the better accommodation of numbers living at a distance; at the same time he manifested his interest by generously offering to procure a carriage for my conveyance. This suggestion led to the organization of another class in that town, under the care of several resident young men. My class was somewhat diminished by the formation of this new one, but continued to have an average number of twelve or fourteen.

The interest of the class, which decreased a little during the intense cold of winter, revived again in the spring, and continued to increase through the summer. At some meetings a very deep solemnity has pervaded the class; and personal conversation has in some instances discovered a tenderness of conscience which encourages the hope that the Lord, who " has made of one flesh all the nations of the earth," does intend to prepare some of these poor souls for his heavenly kingdom.

A girl about twenty years of age, who has long been striving hard, in opposition to many natural obstacles, to learn to read, having made but little or no progress, one day burst into tears and said: " I do want to learn to read my Bible."

Another girl, about the same age, who had made considerable progress in her efforts to read, said, with eyes full of tears: " Oh, how I want to be able to sit down and read *one* chapter in my Bible. But I am almost discouraged, and sometimes think I will give it up." After a little encouragement, she said: "I will begin once more and try harder, for I do want to read my Bible."

The woman mentioned above, who had begun to read with the class, has appeared exceedingly interested ever since the class was organized. She refuses to work out on Wednesday, for she wishes to spend that day at home, so as to devote part of it to her lessons for the Bible class. She often shows much sorrow for sin, and expresses strong desires to become a Christian. Oh, may the Lord renew her heart! This class, which I now leave, I commend to the prayers of those who love the souls of all men, and to the protection of the God of all grace, praying with earnestness that I may meet each member of it in the kingdom of glory.

At nine o'clock Sabbath morning I had a class of the boys of my school in the Sabbath-school at the church. I then rode three miles and held a public service in a large school-house, in what was called the North Parish, reading a printed sermon. In a short time I organized a Sabbath-school, which I superintended in this school-house at the close of the morning service; then in the afternoon we had a Bible service, for which I made very careful preparation. This service became so crowded that the house and entry were full, and many gathered on the outside about the windows. Then at five o'clock in the afternoon I held my Bible class for colored people in the village. This made the Sabbaths of the year very busy days.

A revival of great interest commenced in the North Parish, soon after these various services at the school-house began. As the results of this revival, in a year or two a Congregational church of about sixty-five members, including several who were already professors of religion, was formed. A convenient house of worship was erected a year or two later, at the dedication of which I delivered a written address.

All my half-holidays were spent, after the revival commenced, in visiting among the people of my little parish. And frequently I attended their weekly-prayer-meetings. Some of the most interesting memories of my life are connected with our services among this most appreciative and affectionate people.

In the annual report of the Maine Sabbath-school Union for 1832, the board of managers thus speak of the school here referred to : —

"In the North Parish of Augusta the Sabbath-school embraces almost the entire number of adults and children who usually meet together for worship. The whole history of this church is identified with the history of Sabbath-school operations among them. The exercises of the school have constituted their choicest means of grace and salvation ; and perhaps in no place have the privileges of Sabbath-school instruction been, or can be, more affectionately cherished. Within the year eleven have been converted from three classes, and nine of these are adults who have never, before the last spring, been connected with a Sabbath-school."

In a recent letter from my former and highly respected pupil, Rev. Benjamin Tappan, D.D., of Norridgewock, Maine, he writes : —

My Dear Old Friend and Teacher, Mr. Bullard, — I had quite an unexpected pleasure last evening in receiving and reading your kind letter, which I have read again to-day. I remember well those old Augusta days, the very pleasant addition you made to my father's family ; the great improvement of your teaching in the secular school upon that of your predecessors ; the excellent religious influence you exerted as a teacher in the Sabbath-school and in your social intercourse. The North Parish work I did not, of course, know so much about, except through the report of others. But I can think of it only as a blessing to Augusta that you spent that year there. I know that was my father's and mother's feeling. It must be a matter of great joy and thankfulness to you that you have been enabled to do so much good in your long life.

My year at Augusta was, indeed, a very busy, but, to me, a very enjoyable year.

CHAPTER X.

IN the autumn of 1829, at the close of my year in Augusta, I entered the theological seminary at Andover. I had been looking forward to this institution with very great interest. I had supposed there was no spot on earth much nearer heaven. It would be, I thought, so *easy to be good* there. The very atmosphere, I supposed, would be fragrant with heavenly odors. There I should find a sacred retreat which the great Tempter would never dare to approach.

While there was much in the seminary and its environments that was indeed helpful in the Christian life, I soon found that prayer and watchfulness were not less needed here than in college or any of the walks of life. Wherever the sons of God may be, Satan will be sure to come among them.

While the studies of the seminary were the main thing to occupy my time and thoughts, I felt it a duty and privilege to be doing something, so far as I might, for the good of others. So I at once connected myself with the Sabbath-school of the South Church in the village.

The first year I was the teacher of a class of mothers, and the second year assistant superintendent with the late Rev. Thomas Brainard, D.D., of Philadelphia.

That school was probably one of the largest, if not the largest, in the state. On one Sabbath there were present six hundred and seven persons, including those of all ages from three to about ninety. In one part of the house there were several classes of women, in another several of men; and in the gallery, sweeping around three sides of that great church, were the young men, most of the young men connected with the congregation, and no one of them ever intimated that he was either too old or too wise to be in the Sabbath-school studying the Word of God. And as a result of this general interest in studying the Scriptures, blessing after blessing, rich as could come from heaven, was shed down upon that people.

Once a month notice was given by the superintendent that next Sabbath would be the "contribution day." All were invited to bring at least one cent each. On the contribution day, just before the offerings were taken, I used to go round among some of the smaller scholars and ask them if they had their pennies for the contribution. If any one said he had forgotten to bring one, I would loan him a cent, saying if he thought of it he could bring it to me the next Sabbath. Only a few years ago a lady, who was then a member of a class of eight young girls of from eight to ten years of age, met me and asked if I remembered loaning cents for the contribution to the children who had forgotten to bring them. When informed that I well remembered it, "Well," said she, "I used to leave mine at home on purpose, so as to show you if you loaned me one I should remember to bring it the next Sabbath."

When Dr. Brainard, who was two years my senior in the seminary, left, I was chosen superintendent of this school. It was a very responsible position, and I had labored quite earnestly to prepare myself for it in visiting my corps of teachers and many of the families from which the scholars came. But most unexpectedly I was called to engage in public Sabbath-school work in the state of Maine, of which an account will be given in the next chapter.

One vacation during my course at Andover I was employed, under the appointment of the Massachusetts Sabbath-School Union, which was composed of the Congregational and Baptist denominations of the state, in visiting and addressing eighteen of the churches and schools in the northern part of Worcester County in regard to Sunday-school matters ; and one vacation I was engaged by the friends of this institution in Kennebec County, Maine, in promoting this cause among the churches and schools in that county.

These vacation labors very likely, without such a thought of it on my part, had much to do in preparing me for what has been my life-work.

About this time quite a new and extensive interest was awakened in the cause of Sunday-schools. In 1829, my first year at Andover, a Sabbath-school and Bible class association was formed among the students of the seminary, and a similar one in the divinity school of Yale University, New Haven, Conn. The object of these societies was to collect and diffuse information concerning Sabbath-schools and Bible classes, and to learn the best methods of conducting and extending them.

The association at Andover held frequent meetings, at which papers were read, followed with free discussions on various practical subjects connected with the management of these schools and classes. There were several committees : one of correspondence, whose duty it was to correspond with clergymen and others in all parts of this and foreign lands in regard to the interests of the institution ; one on review, whose duty it was to examine and recommend books for the library ; and one on publication, with which Professor E. A. Park, then a student, and myself were connected, whose duty it was to prepare articles from the communications received by the committee of correspondence and from the papers and discussions of our monthly meetings for the press. Twelve or fifteen such articles were published in *The Sabbath-School Treasury* of the Massachusetts Sabbath-School Union for 1830-31.

The subjects of some of these articles were as follows : —

" How can ministers of the gospel best promote the interests of Sabbath-schools? "

" Mutual instruction."

" What is your mode of teaching? "

" How can Sabbath-schools be made to benefit remote parts of the town? "

" Methods of replenishing the library," etc.

At a meeting of the students of Andover Seminary, June 12, the year previous to the organization of the association, the following resolution was passed : —

Resolved, That we will endeavor to make ourselves acquainted with the best system of Sabbath-school management and instruction and to qualify ourselves in all respects as far as we are able to lend our influence to this cause; and that we consider ourselves obligated to aid, according to the measure of our ability, in promoting its advancement wherever God in his providence may call us.

All these students carried the spirit of this resolution with them into the ministry ; and they were ever the warm friends and supporters of this institution.

Many feel that the students in all our theological seminaries should receive instruction on this subject that shall help to prepare them to give efficiency to their Sunday-schools.

CHAPTER XI.

MY oldest brother, the late Rev. Artemas Bullard, D.D., for eighteen years pastor of the First Presbyterian Church in St. Louis, Mo., was, for four or five years prior to 1832, the secretary of the Massachusetts Sabbath-School Union. The year I was in Augusta he attended the meeting of the General Conference in Maine. In an address in regard to Sunday-schools, he recommended to the churches the employment of an agent to labor in Maine in visiting the schools already established and to organize new ones where needed. He told the people that he would obtain for them the man, if the churches in Maine would raise the money for the necessary expense. In 1830 the board of managers of the Maine Sabbath-School Union. wrote him, reminding him of his promise, and requesting him to send them the agent and, if he could, they wished him to send me.

When my brother proposed this agency to me, my feelings were entirely opposed to it. I did not wish to leave the seminary without completing the usual three years' course. And then, how could I give up the great interest I had anticipated in superintending that important Sabbath-school in Andover?

The question of duty in this matter was one of the most serious that ever had come before me. At the close of my theological course my heart was set upon finding my field of labor at the West. My brother thought that my most direct course to the West was by the way of

Maine; that a few months in this work in the Sabbath-school cause would be the best way to fit myself for the great field at the West.

After much consideration and seeking the advice of wise counselors and especially divine guidance, I accepted the invitation and became the general agent of the Maine Sabbath-School Union. My first expectation was to spend only some six months in this work, and then return and finish my course at Andover. But it was not long before the work became so interesting and its continuance appeared so important, that I was urged by the board to close my connection with the seminary. This I did, and as general agent and corresponding secretary, I continued my labors for the Union three years.

At that time the institution of Sabbath-schools in Maine was comparatively in its infancy. There were only about three hundred schools connected with the Union, in the Congregational and Baptist churches, and not over five hundred in the whole state, containing, perhaps, a total of twenty thousand teachers and scholars.

In describing the work of these three years in Maine, I shall not do better than to repeat a portion of the account given in my "Fifty Years with the Sabbath-schools," published in 1876:—

At the sixth annual meeting of the Union, the first since my connection with it, January, 1832, so important did the work appear that the following resolution was presented, and after a most earnest advocacy, unanimously and with much enthusiasm adopted:—

Resolved, That, relying upon divine assistance, we will establish a Sabbath-school in every town and school district in the state, where it is practicable and advisable, within a year and a half from this time.

During the discussion of this subject, a member of the board of managers offered, in case the resolution should be carried into effect, to give one hundred and fifty dollars towards the expense of the undertaking.

It was understood that it was not generally advisable to establish a school in any district where the children could attend any school already existing; and it was not considered practicable unless it could be accomplished at a reasonable expense of money and labor.

It was comparatively an easy matter, on a pleasant January evening, and in a warm and comfortable church, to pass this resolution, but it was found to be a very different matter to carry it into effect. But this action of the Union deeply stirred the hearts of all the friends of the cause in the state; and it is believed there never has been a period when there was a greater amount of Sabbath-school work done in Maine than during the year and a half contemplated in that resolution.

Early in the spring, though the traveling before the roads were settled was exceedingly difficult, I traversed the state in every direction, visited the auxiliary unions, and held meetings to secure in every county and town committees and individuals who would become responsible for the accomplishment of their portion of the work. Nearly the whole state was thus appropriated to committees and individuals. And a vast amount of labor from voluntary and unpaid agents was secured during the year. Young women were obtained to teach district schools, with special reference to the establishment of Sunday-schools in the towns and neighborhoods where they taught. Merchants were pledged to converse with their customers from adjacent towns or districts, and persuade them, if possible, to see that the work was accomplished in their respective communities. Juvenile sewing circles were formed to help furnish funds for carrying on the enterprise.

It is interesting, at this distance of time, to look back and see the enthusiasm manifested so extensively in this undertaking. Men and women every-where entered into it most heartily. Ten gentlemen took seventeen towns and promised to visit them on the Sabbath, and, so far as it was practicable, to establish schools where they were needed. An aged minister, with whitened locks, pledged himself to carry the resolution into effect in seven different towns, in some of which there never had been a school. The plan he adopted for establishing a school in one of these towns was quite novel and interesting. Having consulted with the minister of the place, and appointed a meeting for the purpose, he took his superintendent and several teachers and went to the meeting. After addressing the people on the subject, he assisted in organizing a school into classes, and choosing the superintendent and teachers. Then, with his superintendent and teachers, he gave the people a practical illustration of their manner of teaching and conducting a Sabbath-school. This was over fifty years ago, and yet was precisely like the Sabbath-school exercise often given at our conventions of the present day. A few weeks after this, two other schools were in operation and arrangements were made to organize two more.

At the close of a meeting at another place, while several gentlemen were consulting together on the work, a young woman offered to assume the responsibility of establishing and conducting a school in a certain district in an adjoining town, where she expected to teach the public school. .

" But if I should not," she said, " it is only four miles and a half, and I can walk out on Saturday, spend the Sabbath in the Sunday-school, and then return on Monday."

She taught the school, as she expected, and also established and sustained a Sunday-school, almost unaided by any one.

" There is such a neighborhood," said a man, " where there must be a Sabbath-school. I don't know whom we can get to go out there. I don't know as there is any one ; but I will see that the work is done." As he finished this remark a woman, perhaps fifty years of age, said : —

" Why won't you let me go to that neighborhood? "

One of the managers of a county union proposed, at their meeting for consultation, that an agent should be employed six months to assist them in redeeming their pledge. He also informed them where no small part of the necessary funds could be obtained.

" There are fifteen or sixteen young ladies," said he, " who have been, or are now, connected with my class in the Sabbath-school, and have all become hopefully pious. Two months ago, they formed themselves into a sewing society, to meet once in two weeks. They have already in their treasury about thirty dollars, and they say they will increase it to seventy-five or one hundred dollars, and give it towards defraying the expenses of an agent in this county, if the board will employ one. They have also pledged themselves to redeem one hour from sleep every morning to work for the cause of Sabbath-schools.

In another county, instead of employing an agent, the pastors of the Congregational churches made an arrangement in the spring for a general exchange, when all were to present the subject of Sabbath-schools to each congregation. In addition to this, each minister was to spend, a few days in some part of the week with the brother with whom he exchanged ; and they two were to go into all parts of the parish, where it was needful, and hold meetings on the subject, to establish, revive, or encourage Sabbath-schools, as the case might require. The effect of this labor was most happy, both upon the ministers and upon the people. The former, from the very fact that they labored in the cause, became more deeply interested in it; while the latter naturally concluded that an object which had taken such strong hold upon the feelings of their ministers must be an important one, deserving their hearty coöperation. These are but a few specimens of the zeal with which men and women all over the state entered into this noble work.

At the next annual meeting it was reported that a great amount of work had been performed, and one hundred new schools had been organized; but much more remained to be done to carry out the resolution than could be accomplished by the general agent alone.

Early in the spring, therefore, I visited the colleges, theological and other seminaries, and clergymen, secured the services for this work of eighteen students and eight or ten ministers, for from one or two to seven weeks each; so that, at the anniversary in January, 1834, it was reported that the objects of the resolution passed in 1832 had been substantially accomplished.

During that year, one hundred and eighty-nine new schools were organized, making the whole number connected with the Union nine hundred and twenty-nine, containing a membership of over thirty-eight thousand.

During the three years of this agency about three hundred new schools were established under my direction. Some of these schools, for the want of the fostering care of the church, in a few months became extinct, but many of them are now among the most flourishing and efficient schools in the state. And there were many men and women who took part in that work who long looked back upon it with no small degree of satisfaction. And there were many laborers in those days — almost threescore years ago — in Maine, who would compare favorably with any of the most zealous and successful Sunday-school workers of the present day.

Soon after the commencement of my agency, the board began to publish a small weekly paper, *The Sabbath-School Instructor*, edited by the secretary, Mr. William Cutter. Through this paper, which was widely taken in the schools and churches, I was able to keep the friends of the Union informed of my work; and also to furnish articles to be read at the Sabbath-school concerts, as well as to address parents, teachers, and children.

The publication of this paper greatly aided in carrying out the resolution. Its importance was constantly discussed and the coöperation of the churches earnestly solicited. The frequent reports from the schools helped to encourage other schools ; and the discussion of the best methods of conducting schools was also very helpful and stimulating.

In order to give me more influence and facility in my agency among the churches, at the suggestion of many of the ministers in Maine, I applied to an association at Augusta, October 25, 1831, and was licensed to preach the gospel, and at the annual meeting of the Union, January 13, 1832, was ordained as an evangelist. The exercises of the occasion were peculiar, inasmuch as they were all more or less directly connected with my special work. The following account of the services appeared in *The Sabbath-School Instructor*, published weekly in Portland, by the Union : —

"Ordained in Portland, on the thirteenth instant, Rev. Asa Bullard, as an evangelist. Introductory prayer by Rev. Adam Wilson, of Portland [Mr. Wilson was the editor of a Baptist paper and a member of the Board of Managers of the Union] ; sermon by Rev. Benjamin Tappan, of Augusta, text, Deut. 31 : 12, 13 (1) ; consecrating prayer by Rev. Jothan Sewall, of Chesterville ; charge by Rev. Dr. Tyler, of Portland ; right hand of fellowship by Rev. Professor Alvin Bond, of Bangor ; address by Rev. Daniel D. Tappan, of Alfred ; concluding prayer by Rev. M. Butler, of the Baptist church, North Yarmouth.

" The exercises of the occasion were appropriate and of a peculiarly interesting character. The sermon exhibited

in a happy and impressive manner the importance of bib-
lical instruction.   Among other topics, the preacher dwelt
upon the Sabbath-school institution, as combining the
most successful means for diffusing a knowledge of the
Bible, and pre-occupying the minds of the rising generation in favor of the sacred truths and pure morality of the
gospel."

Only a week or two before the above occasion, I was
taken very seriously ill with an epidemic then prevailing
in the city, and for a few days was in a critical condition.
At first it was supposed that the ordination could not take
place at the time appointed, but the council had been called
and all who were to take a part in the exercises were present (excepting my brother, Secretary of the Massachusetts
Sabbath-School Union, who was to have given the right
hand of fellowship), and it was thought best to proceed.
The invalid, then slowly convalescent, was bundled up and
carried to the church, and the exercises, after a short and
not very searching examination of the candidate, proceeded.   In the consecrative prayer, Father Sewall, as he
was called, as he laid his hand, tremulous with age, on my
head, tenderly and with choked utterance said :—

"We had feared, O Lord, that we should be called to
follow this thy young servant to the grave, but thou hast
in great mercy rebuked his disease, and art now permitting
us to consecrate him to the work of the ministry, to labor
in thy vineyard."

In February, 1832, the Congregational church and
parish in the town of Bloomfield, Maine, — now Skowhe-
gan, — gave me a unanimous call " to settle within the
gospel ministry."   But there seemed to me to be no
intimation of providence for me to change my field of
labors, and the call was declined.

In some respects the most important and interesting event connected with my worldly and, indeed, my religious life took place during my three years' work in Maine — my marriage. It occurred May 16, 1832, in Amherst, Massachusetts. During my five or six years in Amherst, in my preparatory and collegiate course, I was acquainted with Miss Lucretia G. Dickinson. She and two or three of her young female cousins and associates, then sixteen or seventeen years of age, had but recently become interested in religion and united with the church. It was about the same time and at about the same age that I had myself taken the same important step; so from almost the first week that I entered the town I was brought into acquaintance with this circle of young Christians. My first boarding-place, on entering the academy, was at the home of one of the cousins.

About the close of my third year in college, I thought of teaching a year. This plan was given up, but not till I had lost both my room-mates, with whom I had enjoyed a most pleasant fellowship for three years, and also the chance of a room in the college buildings. This, providentially and, as now is evident, most happily to me, was the means of my obtaining a room and board at the pleasant home of Samuel Fowler Dickinson, Esq., and after nearly a year's residence together in the same house, or, as the adage has it, after we had "summered and wintered each other," we mutually entered into a promised alliance of interests for life.

The three or four years of our betrothal gave us the opportunity of testing each other's fidelity to our mutual pledges, and also of the truth of the proverb that there is "more happiness in anticipation than in participation." But after walking in happy fellowship with my now sainted companion for more than fifty-three years, I can by no means accept the adage.

The following items in regard to her father are gathered from Professor Tyler's " History of Amherst College during its first Half-century " : —

Samuel Fowler Dickinson was born in Amherst, October 9, 1775. He graduated at Dartmouth College in 1795, at the age of twenty. Though the youngest of his class, he received the second appointment. He united with the West Parish Church, and at twenty-one he was chosen one of the deacons, an office which he held nearly forty years. He began the study of theology with an older brother, Rev. Timothy Dickinson, of Holliston, Mass., intending to enter the ministry. But finding he needed a more active life, he turned his attention to the legal profession, and after the usual term of study, established a law office in his native place.

In 1827 he was chosen representative of the town in the general court, and subsequently a member of the Massachusetts Senate.

He was ranked among the best lawyers — perhaps he was the very best lawyer in Hampshire County — and might doubtless have had a seat on the bench if he had continued in the practice of his profession.

Having a family of five sons and four daughters to educate, and at the same time having at heart the general welfare, he, with a few others, established the academy at Amherst. He started the subscription for it. And this academy was the mother of Amherst College, and the college was expressly owing to his suggestion and influence. His steadfastness, perseverance, the self-sacrificing devotion of his time, property, and personal service, gave it success.

As the work of erecting the first building of the college proceeded, and all the available means were used up, Mr. Dickinson would pledge his private property to the bank to obtain money that the work might go on. And when there was no money to pay for the teams to draw the brick, or men to drive them, his own horses were sent for days and weeks till in one season two or three of them fell by the wayside. Sometimes his own laborers were sent to drive his horses, and in an emergency he went himself rather than the work should cease. At the same time he boarded more or less of the workmen, and sometimes paid their wages out of his own pocket, while his wife and daughters toiled to board them. With all the zeal and efforts of numerous friends and benefactors, the work would often have stopped had he not pledged his property till the money could be raised. His own means at last began to fail. His business, which was so large as to require all his time and care, suffered from his devotion to the public. He became embarrassed, and at length actually poor. And in his poverty he had the additional grief of feeling that his services were forgotten, like the poor wise man in the proverb who "by his wisdom delivered the city, yet no man remembered that same wise man."

When Lane Seminary went into operation he was offered a situation as steward, with the oversight and general management of the grounds.

He accepted it and remained at Cincinnati several years, and then accepted a similar situation in connection with the Western Reserve College, at Hudson, Ohio. After a year of great labor and many discouragements, he died at Hudson, April 22, 1838, at the age of sixty-two, in the full possession of his faculties, and in the precious hope of rest and reward in heaven. His body lies in the cemetery at Amherst by the side of the wife of his youth, amid the graves of his relatives and friends, and within sight of the college which he so loved and cherished, and to which he devoted so many years of his life.

The last time I ever saw Squire Dickinson was as we were taking our leave of the paternal home after the wedding ceremony. As he helped his daughter into the carriage, he turned to me and said : —

"I wish I was able to give a fortune with my daughter, but I am sure you will find a fortune in her."

And for the more than fifty-three years we were permitted to walk together in the most endearing of all earthly relations I did, indeed, find a fortune in her.

A small company of relatives and friends accompanied us in carriages about ten miles to a public house in Belchertown, where they provided a lunch, and then, with their kind wishes and farewells and benedictions, left us to pursue our journey. After visiting my old home in Sutton and friends in several other places we made our way to friends in Boston. I purchased a new chaise and a fine orthodox horse at Andover, and thus equipped we journeyed to our new home in Portland.

After spending three weeks in introducing to various friends the stranger I had brought among them, I left her, "a stranger in a strange land," for three weeks' labors in the western counties of the state. My first night was passed in the town of Buxton with the Rev. Mr. Lowing, pastor of the Congregational church in that town. A somewhat amusing incident occurred in connection with this visit. As was the practice very generally in those days in Christian families, they had worship both morning and evening, with reading of the Scriptures. At evening worship the twenty-third chapter of Deuteronomy was read. In reading the twenty-fourth chapter — showing that they were reading in course — in the morning, the fifth verse read thus : "When a man hath taken a new wife, he shall not go out to war, neither shall he be charged with any business; but he shall be free at home one year, and shall cheer up his wife which he hath taken." This was, under the circumstances, surely a very singular coincidence. I inquired, after prayers, if I was not going counter to the Scriptures, and if I ought not to return to my wife. Such a return, I found at the end of my tour, would have cheered up a very lonely bride in that strange city.

I had, in my previous year and a half's labor, visited almost every town in the state. Every-where, among clergymen and laymen, there was manifested the most cordial hospitality. All were frank and open-hearted; and the interest the ministers felt in my work secured for me a special welcome to every parsonage.

The clergyman's house, in those days, was indeed

regarded as the minister's tavern. It was open to all clergymen. Now and then a minister would be found who would call on a perfect stranger for hospitality, giving very strange reasons. One who had been traveling in Maine called on a pastor of one of the large churches in Massachusetts for entertainment during the night; and he gave as a reason for taking such liberty that "he met his brother one day, as they both stopped at the same trough to water their horses." That was many years ago, and such hospitality is not expected at the present day.

The following extract from a letter written during my three weeks' tour in the western part of the state, spoken of above, will show the earnestness and cordiality with which the ministers entered into my work among them : —

The ministers here have almost torn me in pieces. I could not satisfy their wishes for my labors among their people if I could divide myself into twenty agents. To-morrow they are to meet, and then I shall say to them : " Here I am at your disposal for three weeks. Use me just as you can agree." In this way they must assume all the blame, if blame there be, if I do not visit all the places where they may wish my services.

It is exceedingly gratifying to me to hear the ministers and others speak of the number of hopeful conversions and the happy results which have followed my meetings among their people last year. How much grace I do need ! Do not forget me in your prayers.

On my return to Portland I found that our home was not quite what was expected. So, with a small and compact outfit, we made our home for several months in our chaise, traveling sixteen hundred miles through almost the whole state, east of Portland, down to Sebec, Eastport, and Calais, with only the St. Croix River separating us from British territory.

Over all this ground I had been the year before, visiting nearly every town and village, and every-where the greatest interest had been expressed in my work, and wherever I had made my home for a day the warm-hearted, hospitable inmates most cordially invited me to come again and be sure to bring my "better half" with me, so I knew just *where* to stop in every place we visited. And my better half became a fellow-helper in the work, pleading the Sabbath-school cause with the mothers and children at home, while I was holding meetings and laboring among the people outside. Sometimes she was left for a day or two, while I branched off into several adjoining towns or districts. At Calias she was left in a pleasant and hospitable family, while a Mr. Nash, an earnest Sunday-school man of the place, and myself, on horseback (for there were no roads for a carriage), visited Princeton, Alexander, Crofordville, and several other places back in the new country; and held meetings and organized a new school in every place we visited.

In Princeton there were about seventy-five inhabitants, scattered along a road for a mile or more. I called at every house and gave notice of a meeting to be held at a small school-house at two o'clock in the afternoon, where I was to give an address on Sabbath-schools, and if the people became interested, organize one in their town. The wash-tubs and every thing else in the houses and on the farms with which the people were engaged at work were at once put aside; and all the inhabitants, except the mothers with little ones, were at the meeting. After my address, in which all seemed interested, I requested "all who wish to have a Sabbath-school organized, to rise," when all but three young men arose. We aided in choosing the super-intendent and teachers for the school, which was to begin the next Sabbath.

After explaining the whole manner of conducting the school, Mr. Nash told them about a library and informed

them if they would raise five dollars, the Sabbath-school
friends in Calais had authorized him to say that they would
obtain for them ten dollars' worth of good books. And the
money was at once raised on the spot. In one of the
other places we visited, Mr. Nash, instead of saying, as he
meant to have said, that the Calais friends would raise five
dollars for the library, if they would raise the same, said
that "the Calais friends would raise *as much* as they
would." They raised on the spot fifteen dollars, and the
Calais friends could not back out, so the new school
obtained a fine thirty dollar library.

This autumn journey of sixteen hundred miles, while
full of pleasure to the laborers, was apparently full of
interest and profit to the people visited.

This was the only time, in all my life-work in Sunday-
school, that I have ever presumed to take any of my family
with me.

Among the interesting incidents connected with our
journeyings may be mentioned the following :—

We had an interesting experience in a visit to the then
new town of Weld, where the Abbott family for awhile
made their home. The road for miles was new and rough
and through extensive woods where the fires had swept,
and many of the trees were leafless and dead. There
came up a high wind. We were riding with the chaise
turned back, and were in no small apprehension lest some
of the dead trees might fall upon us. Soon we came to a
tree, a foot or so through, that had just fallen directly
across our way. There was no getting round it, and we
had no axe. Having lightened the chaise of its load, I
carefully led the horse over the tree, then turning him one
side, succeeded in rolling one wheel over, without capsiz-
ing the carriage, and then turning him the other way,
rolled the other wheel over.

Weld we found one of the most picturesque townships we had visited in Maine. There were high hills, or broken ridges of mountains, on all sides, excepting on the south, by which we entered. It appeared like a vast crater of a volcano, about twelve miles in diameter, in which quietly reposed the town.

It is well known that the Abbott family have ever been noted for their literary character. And almost every spot in this town bore marks of it in the classical names they had given. The beautiful lake in the center of the valley was called Loch Lomond ; there was Lee Meadow, the Dingle, and the Ben Venue High School. There was no high school, but there was a fine eminence where they proposed that a *high* school should some time be located.

It was said that the members of the Congregational church and society were all on one side of the lake, and the Baptists on the other, so that, not "a great gulf," but "much water," separated them.

Our visit to this romantic town, our meetings in the different societies and districts, and our most hospitable entertainment for some days at the model home of Esquire Abbott, the honored father of these distinguished literary sons, are among our most vivid and pleasant recollections of the State of Maine in those long years ago.

Our last year in Maine we boarded in the family of the late Mrs. Payson, widow of the late Rev. Dr. Payson, whose memory we found most fragrant among all the members of his church and society.

In the family of Mrs. Payson were her two daughters, Louise, afterwards the wife of the late Professor Hopkins, of Williams College, and Elizabeth, afterwards Mrs. Prentiss, and author of "Stepping Heavenward" and several other excellent works.

After two years and eight months of almost unintermitted labor, I became pretty thoroughly tired, not of my work, but in it. I had been almost constantly on the wing, and, like Noah's dove, "found no rest for the sole of my foot." I had traveled between seven and eight thousand miles (five thousand of it with my own horse); preached and given addresses about eight hundred and fifty times ; visited more than a thousand different families ; attended between fifty and sixty public meetings and numerous meetings of committees for consultation. A portion of the time I conducted the correspondence of the Board of Managers, prepared their reports, etc.

At the end of this term of almost three years I addressed to the Board a communication, resigning my connection with the Maine Sabbath-School Union. In answer to this communication, the Board unanimously adopted the following action, January 7, 1834 : —

Rev. Asa Bullard, — While we regret that you feel it to be your duty to terminate your services as general agent of the Maine Sabbath-School Union, it affords us the highest pleasure to express to you our entire approbation of your devoted labors in behalf of the Sabbath-school cause in Maine, and our deep sense of the value and faithfulness of your services.

You will carry with you wherever you may labor in the cause of Christ our best wishes, and our fervent prayers for your success.

Permit us to commend you to the friendship and good offices of all Christians among whom you may be called, in the providence of God, to labor.

By order of the Board of Managers,

A. RICHARDSON, *President.*
WILLIAM CUTTER, *Secretary.*

After being, as I thought, providentially led to give up my early plan of engaging in missionary work in Africa, I became greatly interested in the inviting field for Christian work at the great west. Indeed, I went to

Maine, as a good friend suggested, as the "most direct way to the west." A year or two of this Sabbath-school work in Maine, it was thought, would be the best preparation for what I then supposed was to be the scene of my life-work.

Just before resigning my connection with the Maine Sabbath-School Union, as mentioned above, Rev. Stephen Peet, agent of the American Seamen's Friend Society, for the inland and western waters, under date of Cleveland, Ohio, November 26, 1833, wrote a long letter in regard to his work, from which I give the following extracts : —

Dear Brother, — Having learned that your thoughts have been turned towards the west, I wish to direct your attention to a field of usefulness to which, I am informed by your friends, you are in a good degree adapted — a field long neglected, but vastly important, and which is now white for the harvest. I refer to the inland waters of our country and the multitudes of seamen and boatmen who are engaged upon these waters.

After giving a minute account of the great need of Christian labor among this interesting class, and of what had already been accomplished in erecting chapels and employing preachers, establishing libraries and schools for their benefit, he says : —

The chaplain at Cleveland will be the pastor of a congregation reaching through the center of this state, a distance of 343 miles, and over all Lake Erie, from Buffalo to Detroit. There is a population of perhaps two or three hundred in the vicinity of the water who, perhaps, never entered a place of worship, to be looked up and brought out. There are all the boatmen on the canal to be visited and furnished with Bibles, etc., and the hundreds and thousands of travelers and emigrants who are filling up the great valley.

The question now, dear brother, is, Will *you* enter this field and engage in the business of preaching and laboring among the seamen and boatmen of the western waters? I have conversed with your brother at Cincinnati [my brother was then district secretary of the American Board of Foreign Missions for the valley of the Mississippi] on the subject. He says he thinks you will come, and that you *ought* to come. I wish you to occupy the station at Cincinnati, Cleveland, Buffalo, or Louisville, to be determined after your arrival, etc.

This seemed to me a "Macedonian call," and I readily took it into serious consideration ; and when I had so far accepted it that Mr. Peet probably supposed I was on the way thither, I was most unexpectedly "let" at Boston by a call to what has proved to be my life-work, to become the secretary and general agent of the Massachusetts Sabbath-school Society, now called the Congregational Sunday-School and Publishing Society.

After very serious and prayerful consideration, and much marveling at the manner in which providence had several times so obviously disposed of what I proposed, I accepted the invitation and entered upon the service for the Society March 1, 1834. And the work has been to me most congenial ; and I have not since, during all these years, desired for one moment any other field of Christian labor. Not that there may not be more important ones, yet for me none more promising. In no other field is one brought so closely into connection with home life. In no work does the laborer meet with warmer sympathy than that connected with parents and children.

CHAPTER XII.

MY life-work, for fifty-four years prior to the first of
March, 1888, has really been with the Congregational Sunday-School and Publishing Society. And a brief
summary of this work may be interesting before entering
upon the details.

There is not a person now connected with any of the
offices of the Society, or the Board of Managers, nor
among the employees, who was connected with the
Society in any way when I entered upon my labors for
it, March 1, 1834.

In my work as general agent for nearly fifty-seven
years, including my three years in Maine, I have made
over 4,000 visits in 1,300 towns and parishes, preached and
given addresses 7,729 times, and traveled about 300,000
miles, not including a tour of three months in Europe.
With the exception of three western tours, all this travel
has been in comparatively short journeys, mostly in New
England. I have attended annually more or less public
meetings, state and county conferences and associations of
churches, Sabbath-school conventions, festivals, etc., in
different parts of the country. In connection with these
visits, I have probably addressed more than two million
persons, perhaps more than eight hundred thousand different persons, and a large portion of them many times.

In my connection with this Society I edited every
number of its monthly periodical, *The Sabbath-School*

THE WELL-SPRING

Understanding as a Well-Spring of Life.—Prov. 16. 22.

Published Weekly, BY THE MASSACHUSETTS SABBATH SCHOOL SOCIETY.   Edited by Rev. Asa Bullard

VOL. 3   BOSTON, FRIDAY, JANUARY 8, 1864   NO. 1.

The best Gift.

The beautiful Garment.

THE WELL-SPRING

Understanding as a Well-Spring of Life.—Prov. 16. 22.

Published Weekly, BY THE MASSACHUSETTS SABBATH SCHOOL SOCIETY.   Edited by Mrs. Asa Bullard

VOL. 1   BOSTON, FRIDAY, JANUARY 17, 1851   NO. 1.

George and his Bible.

The lamb.

Visitor for ten years; was assistant editor of *The Congregational Visitor* for three years; and edited, or prepared, every number of its weekly periodical, *The Well-Spring,* over forty years, till April 25, 1884. For many years over sixty thousand copies of *The Well-Spring* per week were published.

I was the corresponding and recording secretary of the Society, of the Board of Managers, and of the Sabbath-school Publishing Committee, and for several years of the Theological Publishing Committee also. I prepared, while acting Secretary, all but five or six of the annual reports of the Society, and all the quarterly reports of the Sabbath-school Committee and the Committee on Agencies. I wrote numerous circulars, letters to Sabbath-schools and juvenile societies, and other public documents. For several years I read all the manuscripts for books, prepared those that were accepted by the committees for publication for the press, and read all the proofs.

To every Sabbath-school that would contribute to the Society from twenty-five to one hundred and fifty dollars annually for its missionary work we promised a letter to be read at its concert. These letters were from our missionaries or Sabbath-school friends, or I wrote them myself. From one hundred to one hundred and fifty copies of these letters were sent every month to as many schools. This was continued for eighty concerts. I wrote or compiled for publication by the Society about forty of its 18mo books, containing over four thousand pages; thirty-six 32mo books, containing eight hundred pages; and numerous cards. I made it my duty and pleasure to perform whatever other labors I could make of service to the Society in its work in behalf of the cause of Sabbath-schools.

At the end of forty years a new Secretary was appointed,

and I was chosen Honorary Secretary and relieved from a large portion of my accustomed labors. A committee of the Board of Managers, of which the Rev. J. H. Means, D.D., of Dorchester, was chairman, appointed to consider the case of the former Secretary, reported, May 14, 1875, as follows : —

That the Board recall with gratitude the earnest and effective labors of the former Secretary, who for forty-one years has stood before the churches as a prominent advocate of the Sabbath-school cause, and has stimulated by his addresses a great multitude of teachers and scholars in all parts of the land.

That, although his relations to the Society are now changed by the appointment of another as Secretary, it is desirable that his services be still retained in presenting the work and claims of the Society before Sabbath-schools and churches as opportunity may permit, and in rendering such other service as the Board may direct ; and that his title be Honorary Secretary.

My services commenced with the Society in its infancy. It was organized May 31, 1832, and I prepared the annual report for the second anniversary, May 29, 1834. At the close of the first year, ending May 30, 1833, the whole business of the Depository was less than eight thousand dollars.

The objects of the Society, according to the second article of its constitution, were "to promote the opening of new, and the increase and prosperity of the existing, Sabbath-schools ; to form depositories for supplying Sabbath-schools with suitable books, on the lowest terms possible ; to stimulate and encourage each other in the moral and religious instruction of children and others" ; so that the Society commenced organizing new Sabbath-schools and aiding destitute ones, especially at the west, from its beginning ; and the amount of donations from the Sunday-schools for this purpose for the first year was $690.47.

At the close of forty years, when a new Secretary was appointed, the business of the Depository for the previous year was not far from $140,000. The amount of donations for our benevolent work was over $8,000, and it was distributed in books and papers in three hundred and thirty-three different needy places.

During these forty years it is estimated that the business of the Society was at least $2,500,000, and the amount of charitable contributions that the Society expended, mostly in books and periodicals for organizing and maintaining Sabbath-schools, at least $200,000.

The missionary work of the Society, in visiting and organizing schools, till within a few years was almost wholly through voluntary agents. Home missionaries were ready to do this work within a reasonable distance from their churches, if the Society would provide them with the libraries and Sabbath-school helps that were needed. Some missionaries, with their helps, organized and sustained six or eight schools. One missionary voluntarily visited several counties around his especial field of labor, and organized over thirty new schools.

For several years the Society employed six or eight paid missionaries, among whom was the well-known lay evangelist, Mr. K. A. Burnell. And the annual reports of the Society will show that a most important work was accomplished from year to year.

The great difficulty in this part of our work was the want of funds. A large part of the schools that contributed to the Society wished their contributions to go to specific schools, so that they could receive letters from the schools aided.

I have now a letter from the late Rev. Henry Ward Beecher, dated Lawrenceburg, Ind., January 25, 1838, acknowledging the gift of a library from the Society for his Sabbath-school, which he superintended. This letter was to be sent to the schools that contributed the money.

The Shorter Catechism.

IN 1835 I came across a book entitled "Anecdotes on the Shorter Catechism." As the study of this catechism, so common in my early days, seemed to have died out, I conceived the plan of publishing one question of the catechism with the answer, the proof-texts, and one of the anecdotes in this book, in *The Sabbath-School Visitor* each month, in order to revive, if possible, the study of this catechism of my childhood. I had published only two or three questions before letters began to come, asking, "What has become of the catechism? Why is it not studied, as formerly, in our families and schools?"

About this time the late Rev. David Sanford, then pastor of the Congregational church in Dorchester village, offered, if our Society would publish a cheap edition of the catechism, to take five hundred copies. In about two weeks the Society published five thousand. A short time after this we published it with the proof-texts; then we published the "New England Primer," and then a book called "Exercises on the Shorter Catechism."

Soon a very general interest was awakened on the subject in families and in Sabbath-schools. Superintendents and pastors began to offer Bibles to all who would commit it to memory. In many cases more than a hundred Bibles were required to meet the offer. It cost the superintendent of a school in West Springfield, Mass., over seventy-five dollars to redeem his pledge. Within fifteen years the Society published and sold, in its various forms, probably not less than half a million copies of the catechism. The influence I was thus providentially permitted to exert, in reviving the study of this excellent compendium of truth, I regard as among the most important events of my life.

Visit of One Thousand Teachers to New York.

IN August, 1855, the governors of some of the public charitable institutions in New York invited the Sabbath-school teachers in Massachusetts to visit Blackwell's and Randall's Islands. It was regarded as a religious enterprise, undertaken with a view to advance the kingdom of Christ. After many meetings for consultation and due arrangement, about one thousand teachers embarked on a steamer on Monday afternoon, September 24, for New York.

After breakfast and a few exercises, almost two thousand children from the various asylums and other institutions for orphans, half-orphans, the friendless, the deaf and dumb, etc., who are supported by the charities of New York, were gathered at the palace. The children of the different institutions were all arranged in squares like patchwork, by themselves, and all arrayed in the dresses peculiar to each institution. One square I called "polished ebony" because it was composed of colored children.

At this meeting, which was attended by the Sunday-school superintendents and teachers of New York and Brooklyn, and many of the clergymen and members of the churches, there were addresses of welcome, responses, etc.

One of the most interesting scenes of the occasion was the appearance before the great audience of Bessy Rourke, — a little child of about six years of age, — who gave a "History of the Five Points Mission," and pointed out the picture of the famous Old Brewery of that locality. At the close of the beautiful and affecting address of this little girl, I was called upon to respond.

The reception given to the visitors from Boston, our visits to the various asylums and reformatory institutions, our meeting with the Sabbath-school friends in Brooklyn, and all the addresses were full of interest and inspiration.

Every thing connected with this event was adapted to magnify the influence and importance of the institution we represented.

This visit of one thousand teachers to New York led to the holding of Sunday-school conventions, which have now become so common.

Visits to the Army.

THE Congregational Sunday-School and Publishing Society, in connection with various other benevolent and philanthropic organizations, during our late war engaged in the work of furnishing the soldiers with reading. The Society prepared a box of six books in uniform style, called " The Soldier's Library," of which large numbers were sent to the army. I compiled a book called " The Soldier's Diary," and a " Book for Leisure Moments," that was widely distributed among the soldiers. Some very interesting cases were reported where fallen soldiers were identified by this book found in their possession. I also edited half a dozen small 32mo books : " The Discharged Soldier," " Hope for the Lost," " Colonel Armine Mountain," " Rest for the Soul," etc., which were published by the Society and widely circulated in the army.

I made two visits to the Potomac and James River armies for the purpose of gathering information that would aid me in presenting the subject of " reading for the soldiers " to the churches, and taking collections for the object. The Christian Commission gave me a commission that permitted me to visit the different armies as a preacher, while gathering the desired information.

In my first visit I was in Washington at the time of the second inauguration of President Lincoln. I spent a day at Annapolis among the five hundred officers and fifteen hundred soldiers who had just arrived from their sufferings in Salisbury Prison.

In the evening a large number of them left, on a furlough, to visit their friends, mostly in New England, and I started with them. At Philadelphia we changed cars, and I tried to get into one of the last two cars, filled with soldiers. I wanted to be with them and help to cheer them on the way. But the cars were so full no place could be found.

About two o'clock on that disastrous night, we overtook a disabled engine of a freight train. While we were thus detained, and, as it was said, "with no signal out," we were run into by an express train. The last two cars were telescoped and the engine of the express train was driven two thirds through those cars, mangling the poor soldiers most fearfully. A large number were killed or wounded! We had to break through the cars with axes to get the soldiers out, and their overcoats were saturated with the scalding steam in which they were enveloped. It was the most heart-rending scene I ever witnessed, and, but for the ordering of a kind providence, I should have been among the sufferers. How strange that those poor soldiers, who had just escaped the horrors of a rebel prison, should so soon meet such a fearful scene of mutilation and death !

In connection with this visit, with some thirty members

of Congress and others, I had the pleasure of visiting our soldiers at Bud's Ferry, and dining with General Hooker. We went in the steamer Yankee, the flag-boat of the Potomac flotilla, as far as Mattawoman Creek. There we took a smaller boat called the Stepping Stone, often mentioned in connection with the war. From there we were carried to General Hooker's quarters, several miles in wagons over a new corduroy road. While going up the Mattawoman Creek, we could see the smoke of the rebel camp three miles distant at Cockpit Point. While looking at it, we saw the smoke and heard the report of two shots from that camp. On reaching Bud's Ferry, I found that a shell had fallen within twenty rods of the First Massachusetts Regiment; the shell which I saw did not burst. The second shell burst very near the Eleventh Massachusetts, and I have a piece of it which I brought home as a relic. At the dress parade of the First Massachusetts, Colonel Cowden called on me for an address, in which I gave as one reason for not going into the war, my fear that the rebels would mistake my white head for a flag of truce.

This visit was on a Saturday, and on Sunday morning it was found that the rebels had fled.

In my visit to the James army I had the pleasure of lunching with the commanding officer, General Devens, and several of his staff officers. It was the day of the capture of Wilmington. The general issued a proclamation of the fact to his soldiers, and ordered a salute on the good news. He gave me the privilege of carrying the order, on my way to the colored regiments of his army. The colored troops received the news with the most uproarious excitement and enthusiasm, and cried out : —

"Bres the Lord ! — Wish it was Richmond ! "

I visited Bermuda Hundred, at one time the headquarters of General Butler, and also the famous Dutch Gap. The agent of the Sanitary Commission, who kindly loaned me his horse to visit this noted spot, requested me to leave the horse some distance from the gaps, as rebels two or three miles off were wont to throw shells if they saw visitors there. So while I went and examined the place, I hitched the horse out of danger.

At Deep Bottom I spent a very dark and stormy night alone in a tent of the Sanitary Commission, which was within a few miles of Richmond, and where was often heard the guns of those on picket. A part of this night I spent writing my "Editorial Correspondence," for *The Well-Spring.* During this visit I traveled about fifteen hundred miles ; preached or gave addresses in chapels of the Christian Commission, in hospitals, gunboats, and schools of the freedmen, sixteen times ; and held personal conversations with soldiers in the cars, steamboats, hospitals, camps, forts, and by the wayside.

It was very pleasant to me in both of these visits to meet so many of the colored people at Washington and other places, and to attend their meetings and listen to their strange and excited manner of worship. At a meeting in Washington, I heard three men and three women pray. They were very fervent, and all made use of the same expressions ; as that "the Lord would come over the mountains of their sins," and that they might not "get within gun-shot of the devil." One young woman, who was quite diffident, prayed for her sister, that the Lord would help her in bringing up her children ; and then she prayed for her husband, "that we may dwell together like two loving doves upon the same bough."

At first I said to myself: " Though that is a beautiful expression, it is not a good figure, because doves never light on boughs;" but in a moment it occurred to me, "This means the turtle-doves," of which the woods at the South are full.

Very soon after my second visit, Richmond fell and the war was closed, and all the interesting facts I had gathered were now, of course, of no avail in my work.

International Sunday-School Convention.

In May, 1875, I had the pleasure of attending and taking part in an international Sunday-school convention at Baltimore. The most popular Sunday-school speakers of the country and of the Provinces and Europe were present, and during the three days' sessions, subjects of great practical interest were discussed.

My Interest in Children.

I have always felt a peculiar interest in children. I never meet them by the way or in public conveyances without feeling myself drawn towards them. My custom for many years has been to have cards and little books to present to such as I have the opportunity. And it is now a very common thing to meet men and women, in all circumstances in life, who remind me of a little book or card they received from me when they were children. And many a one often adds with interest : "And I have got it yet."

It has always seemed very strange that little ones, when well-behaved, can be repulsive to any one. Some years ago I had a correspondence with a woman on this subject, which was so peculiar that the substance of it may interest others.

In an address at a Sabbath-school convention, I expressed interest in the young by saying I thought heaven would be a poor place for one to live who did not love children. About a fortnight afterwards a young woman, an entire stranger, who happened to be present, having learned my name and address, wrote me a letter. Having repeated the above remark, she said : —

Now, Mr. Bullard, I do not love children. They are repulsive to me as a general thing, and I want to ask you if, on that account, I must be excluded from that happy place? I read in the Bible, " Repent and believe on the Lord Jesus Christ and thou shalt be saved." Nothing is there said about loving children as being essential to salvation. Since I was a child myself I have wished to have as little to do with children as possible. I have been told that I ought to cultivate a love for children, but what would such a love amount to? With me, love for any one must spring up spontaneously within me, or is good for nothing. Perhaps it is wrong for me to feel like this, but what can I do? I merely ask, as a great favor, that you will write me a few words in explanation of what you said. I must, indeed, despair of salvation if that is one of the conditions.

In reply to this strange letter, among other things I said : —

Must not heaven be a poor place for people who do not love children, unless their feelings are changed? Suppose angels and saints are *here* " repulsive " to a person. Unless there is a change of feeling in this respect, would not heaven — where there will be so many saints and angels — be a " poor place " for that person?

There will certainly be multitudes of children in heaven. The Saviour says, " Of such is the kingdom of heaven ; " and " Except ye repent and become as little children " — as those that are so " repulsive " to you — " ye cannot see the kingdom of God." Then, it is said, "Unless we have the Spirit of Christ we are none of his." But Christ loved little children, and *took them in his arms* and blessed them. They were not repulsive to him. He was displeased with his disciples, to whom they were so " repulsive " that they rebuked those who brought them to him that he might bless them.

I did not say that any one would be excluded from that happy place on account of not loving children; but only that it would be a "poor place" for such. If children are "repulsive" to you, and you "wish to have as little to do with them as possible," I should think you would want the Saviour, who is preparing a place among the "many mansions" for his people, to prepare one for you, with "No ADMITTANCE TO CHILDREN" on the door, to make it really heaven to you.

Would not a conservatory or a flower-garden be a poor place for one who does not love flowers — to whom they are "repulsive"? I can as readily conceive of a person who does not love flowers as one who does not love children.

I said at that Sabbath-school meeting that no floral exhibition could be more beautiful than that crowd of smiling, happy children. Can it be that those children were "repulsive" to you? Was that a repulsive scene when they sung so sweetly those beautiful songs?

When I speak of children in heaven of course I mean well-behaved children, and I do not know that any others are ever admitted to that blissful home.

What a world this would be without any children! It would be like blotting out all of the stars from our evening skies, and like sweeping away every sweet flower from the meadows and the hillsides.

The prophet, in speaking of the new Jerusalem, says that "the streets were full of boys and girls playing in the streets thereof."

Old People's Day.

REV. WM. J. BATT, late of Stoneham, Mass., now chaplain at the Reformatory, Concord, used to have once a year what he called "Old People's Day." All the old people of his congregation and, indeed, of the town were invited to his church at an afternoon service especially for them. Mr. Batt usually invited some elderly minister to be with him and take part in the services of the day.

At the "Old People's Day" in 1881, I was invited to be with Mr. Batt. The house was quite full on the occasion. There were sixty people present who were over sixty years of age, and twenty-five who were eighty years of age or more. A bouquet was presented to each of these twenty-five. They arose, as their names were called, and received the bouquets as they were presented by the hands of children. At the close of the meeting one of those addressed said : "It knocked twenty years right off from my age."

Perhaps it may not be improper to give the following account of the services of that day, which Mr. Batt published : —

The day passed very pleasantly indeed. Rev. Mr. Bullard's sermon in the forenoon was upon the true method and spirit of studying the Bible, in order to the growth of noble character. It was one of the most remarkable sermons preached in any pulpit that day, we venture to say. The preacher was seventy-seven years old and in no way that we could see asking the least indulgence of his hearers on account of his age. There was indeed only the least possible suggestion that he was old. His hair was abundant, white and not gray. Quite tall in figure, he stood up almost like an arrow for straightness. . . . His voice was clear and strong and was heard easily every-where in the house. Emphasis vigorous, matter excellent, style finished. The sermon was delivered without any notes and yet was reasonably brief. Mr. Bullard's address in the afternoon was very felicitous.

A good audience was present in the evening to hear Mr. Bullard's account of the World's Sabbath-school Convention in London, to which he was a delegate. It was full of instruction and was very greatly enjoyed.

After reaching home at night, Mr. Bullard was asked if he would take a cup of tea, or what he would like for refreshments. The old man of seventy-seven, who had taught a Bible class and spoken at three services, replied: "Nothing, unless it is another meeting."

Almost all of this long ministerial life has been spent in the Sabbath-school work. Young people come up in sets. We may reckon five years to a set. Youth do not go much beyond that limit of difference

of ages in their intimate associations.   As often as once in about that
period of time a new set of young folks comes upon the stage.   In this
way of reckoning, Mr. Bullard, as a writer of books, as an editor, as a
director on a large scale of the religious instruction of the young, has
powerfully molded five or ten generations of youth!   What a life to
look back upon!   What a life for other men to honor!   And not really
old yet!

Fiftieth Anniversary.

At the regular quarterly meeting of the managers of the
Society the following action was taken : —

On the first day of March, 1884, our revered and beloved father,
Rev. Asa Bullard, reached the fiftieth anniversary of his election to
office in this Society.   The length of his term of service is believed
to be unprecedented in the history of similar Sunday-school and
publishing organizations.   The Board of Managers, therefore, desire,
first of all, to recognize devoutly the good hand of our God upon his
servant, and to give thanks for that gracious providence which raised
up, so early in the history of Sunday-schools, a man richly endowed
with gifts of mind and heart for the twofold and difficult work of
providing a proper Sunday-school literature, and of awakening an
intelligent and profound interest throughout and beyond New England
in the religious education of the young.   The members of the Board
also desire to extend to Mr. Bullard their fraternal and hearty congratulations upon his completion of so protracted a period of service,
and, speaking not only for themselves, but also for the thousands of
Christian people to whom his name is familiar as a household word,
to assure him of their appreciation of his eminently faithful, wise, and
successful labors through all these years for Christ and his kingdom.
Their prayer is that his youthfulness of spirit, which is still unabated,
may be immortal, and that the favor of God, which has been so long
and bountifully bestowed upon him, may be still more abundant and
also everlasting.   In view of the faithful labors of Mr. Bullard, continued now for half a century in the service of this Society, the Board
deem it fitting to adopt the following resolution : —

Resolved, That Mr. Bullard deserves to be relieved, and for the
future is relieved, of all editorial labor; but that he be retained in the
service of this Society, and his salary be $600, with the request that
he will continue, as opportunity is given him, to address Sunday-

schools, churches, and other assemblies, in behalf of the work of the Congregational Sunday-School and Publishing Society.

The editor of *The Pilgrim Teacher*, in referring to this action of the Board, says : —

The case of Rev. Asa Bullard is doubtless unprecedented in the fact that he has now for fifty years been the official representative of a Sunday-school society, presenting its claims earnestly and effectively during all this period in the various pulpits of the denomination throughout the land, especially in New England. His services in this line are still in active demand, and there was a long period of years when the call for him from all directions was far greater than he could answer. Though now well advanced, he is still very active, and there are few men of any age who can perform such service more acceptably than he. Mr. Bullard has done and is still doing a great and important work. He keeps up with the times remarkably well, and always has a wonderful freshness for a man of his years.

A pastor, in a local paper, writes under the following head : —

A VETERAN IN SUNDAY-SCHOOL WORK. — March 1, 1834, Rev. Asa Bullard was appointed Secretary of the Massachusetts Sabbath-School Society, now called the Congregational Sunday-School and Publishing Society. From that time till now he has been actively engaged in the service of the Society, giving the labors of a long life to advance the interest of Sunday-schools and the teaching of the Word of God. January 1, 1844, *The Well-Spring* was started, of which Mr. Bullard was the editor; and he still assists in preparing its pages. Every number for forty years has passed through his hands. This continuous service of half a century has hardly a parallel in the history of benevolent societies. Fifty years of labor for children and youth, by voice and pen, is a privilege rarely granted to any one man. A generation has sprung up and passed away since he began his work. He is yet hale and vigorous, and his voice is often heard in the churches, where he is always welcome. This is written, of course, without his knowledge; but we know that the many thousand boys and girls who have heard him speak, many of whom are gray-haired now, will wish for him yet many years of health and usefulness.

Sunday-School Superintendents' Union.

SIX or seven years ago the Congregational Sunday-schools of Boston and vicinity formed a union for mutual benefit. It includes superintendents, present and past, and assistants. Meetings are held monthly. An hour is given to social intercourse, after which there is a collation; then an hour and a half or two hours are spent in an opening devotional service and a discussion of some practical subject connected with the Sunday-school work. This is opened by a paper or address of about twenty minutes, by some one chosen by the executive committee. These meetings are very stimulating and instructive. At the close of the spring meetings, one is held in June, called the Ladies' Meeting, at which the members can invite their lady friends, and a public meeting in the church follows the collation, at which there are addresses usually by clergymen.

At a meeting in 1883, the president invited me, as a guest, to be present. In the course of the meeting one of the members, after some pleasant remarks about a venerable man he used to know when a boy, moved that "Mr. Bullard be chosen as an honorary member of the Union." Another member seconded the motion with some very pleasant remarks, and I was chosen by a rising vote.

This I regard as a great honor and as one of the most complimentary acts ever rendered me. After acting as chaplain at the table a year or two, I have been elected as "Chaplain of the Union for life"!

Sabbath-schools Forty Years Ago.

The work of the farmer when I was a boy was a hand-to-hand work. There were none of the labor-

saving machines and various facilities, now so numerous,
to lighten the toil of the husbandman. The fork then
used was almost as much as a boy twelve years old could
lift. Now that article is almost light and delicate enough
for a table-fork. The farmer now rides to plow, to
harrow, to sow, to reap, to mow, to rake, etc.

The difference in the Sabbath-school work forty years
ago and now is almost as great. Then it was truly a
hand-to-hand work. There were no "helps over hard
places," none of the numerous — perhaps too numerous —
helps that are now provided for superintendents and
teachers to make their work comparatively easy and
efficient.

And yet any one who will examine my volume, " Fifty
Years with the Sabbath-schools," will no doubt be as-
tonished, as I was in preparing it, to see how little there
is in the Sabbath-school work of to-day that is really
new. A lady in Kansas writes : —

"I have read your 'Fifty Years with the Sabbath-
schools' with both pleasure and profit, being constantly
startled by the thought that what we are pleased to call
'new methods' are not new."

Now, take the teachers' meeting. Forty years ago
it was extensively observed, and was regarded as the
thermometer of a school. It was not a meeting to
study the lesson so much as to compare and harmonize
views and aid each other in the best mode of teaching
it to the scholars. A boy twelve years old wrote a com-
position to be read at the concert, on "The Importance
of the Teachers' Meeting," and illustrated his subject
by the fact that one Sabbath he heard three teachers — his own, the one before him, and the one behind
him — give three different answers to the same question ;

and he thought they ought to come together and try to teach alike.

The concert was extensively observed forty years ago, and was every-where spoken of as the largest and most interesting meeting held, as it is now. It was a meeting for prayer, singing, recitation of hymns and Scripture, and addresses. It was not so much an exhibition as it is in some schools at the present day; but it was the children's meeting, and they came even from a distance the coldest winter evenings. As long ago as the concert was held on Monday evening, at East Boston; on that evening there was a display of fireworks, firing of guns, etc., in the vicinity of the vestry, and yet most of the older pupils of the school, boys and girls, came in and were quietly seated through the whole exercises of the evening, apparently unmoved by the roar of the cannon and the blaze of the rockets without. We can hardly find an example of more interest in the concert at the present day.

Forty years ago there was no exercise in which the children so much delighted as in singing. Yet there were then few hymn and tune books but those used in the church. In Taunton, a hymn suited to the capacities of the children was chalked on a blackboard — yes, a *blackboard* forty-five years ago ! — and committed to memory by the whole school. This was sung at the concert to a simple tune adapted to the words, and, said the superintendent in his report : " If the Sabbath-school room may ever be said to resemble 'a little heaven below,' it was while the hundred youthful voices united in a song of praise." You might often hear aged fathers and mothers exclaim, after a concert was over : " Did you ever hear any thing like it ? How the little creatures did sing ! "

More than fifty years ago adult classes began to be formed quite generally in the schools in New England. It soon became common to receive reports that a large portion of the church and congregation were connected with the school. In the report of the Massachusetts Sabbath-School Society for 1841, it is stated that in 226 schools in Massachusetts were 11,692 scholars over eighteen years of age, or an average of over fifty in each school. The pastor in Conway, with a congregation of three hundred or four hundred, counted but eleven of his people who did not enter the school at the close of the morning service.

"Mission," or "neighborhood," or "branch" schools, as they were called, were then common. In country towns then, as now, such schools were not usually for poor children or foreigners, but for those who were too distant to attend the school at the church. Some churches sustained several such schools. One church in Fall River for many years sustained seven such schools from one to three miles from the church.

Some forty years ago one church in Boston asked: "What shall we do for the neglected children and youth in our city? Shall we form mission schools, as some of the churches are doing, or shall we try to gather these neglected ones into our own school?"

The decision was to gather them into their own school and seat them with their own children. And the result was that the school in one year and a half was increased from one hundred and fifty to three hundred and fifty. Of the infant class of about one hundred children all but fifteen or twenty were gathered in from the streets. A class of eighteen Swedes was gathered, thirteen of whom in a year and a half were converted and united with the church. The pastor said of them: "They learned the 'language of Israel' before they had learned our own language."

Visiting scholars at their homes was very common. One teacher in Hopkinton traveled on foot nineteen miles on Fourth of July, 1841, while others were spending the day in pleasure-seeking, to visit the members of his class.

Reciprocal visits by persons chosen for the purpose to address the concert in neighboring schools and interchange of letters to be read at the concert were quite common forty or fifty years ago.

The most important and marked feature in the Sabbath-school work forty years ago was that the chief end with most teachers seemed to be the conversion of the scholars. Sixty-three schools in Massachusetts in 1841 reported 1,622 hopeful conversions during the year; and twenty-seven of those converts the same year commenced preparing for the ministry. Ninety members of the school in Hopkinton and eighty in Holden were that year converted. In Hopkinton every class was visited and from three to seven in some classes converted. A whole class of seven men, from thirty to forty-four years of age, formed a year before, were all converted. In a class of nineteen young men fourteen were converted. A teacher who wrote a note to her scholars every week soon rejoiced over the conversion of six of them. Another teacher, who requested her scholars at a certain hour every day to pray for their own salvation, hoped that five were soon converted. It was common to hear of the conversion of whole classes.

The pastor in West Needham, now Wellesley, reported in 1841 that there were not more than three or four in the whole school over ten years of age who were not either indulging hopes or anxious for their souls. The district school near by was like a Sabbath meeting. At noon the girls went by themselves to a neighboring building, and spent the time in prayer and reading the Bible ; and the boys went into another place for the same purpose. The boys had a weekly prayer-meeting by themselves at the dwellings of their parents ; and besides this two or three seldom met together without prayer. Their voices were often heard in prayer, not only in their retired chambers, but also in barns and sheds and ships. " I am sometimes filled with wonder," said the pastor. " I never witnessed any thing like it. I can not doubt that they are sincere. Forty-two are now hoping. I rejoice, and yet I rejoice with trembling."

This is a sample of the Sabbath-school work quite general forty and fifty years ago.

Several Calls to Other Fields of Labor.

IN 1838, my brother, Rev. Artemas Bullard, then pastor of the First Presbyterian Church in St. Louis, Missouri, wrote me as follows : —

" My church has just sent off a strong colony to form a second church. Half the wealth of my church goes, and more than half of its pious strength. It is a choice draft. They have a man engaged only till spring, then the church will wish to call a pastor. I wish it might be your duty to come and be its pastor."

It would have been very pleasant to have been associated with my brother, as a pastor, in that growing city. But I did not " see it my duty " to accept a call, had a formal one been extended to me.

A few years after this my brother wrote, in behalf of the Bible cause for the valley of the Mississippi, a very earnest invitation for me to become the Secretary and

General Agent of that cause. This invitation was warmly urged by my father-in-law, Samuel Fowler Dickinson, Esq., then connected with the Lane Theological Seminary at Cincinnati. Among the inducements presented for me to accept this invitation, was the fact that the field was the *whole valley of the Mississippi*, while my present field of labor was *only New England!* Just as though any one could properly cultivate either. And besides the field of the Massachusetts Sabbath-School Society, was the Congregational churches throughout the country.

And then again, some years later, a similar call was made for me to engage in the tract cause for the west.

As inviting as these fields appeared, I could see no good reason for leaving a work of sufficient importance to engage the best energies of any one ; and a work, too, in which I had become very deeply interested, and that was so in accord with all my feelings. And I have never seen any occasion to regret my decision. The Sabbath-school work is the one to which, in the providence of God, I was first called, and I have been most happy in giving to it my life.

Several years after this, a member of the Board of the American Sunday-School Union wrote me, inquiring what would induce me to leave the Society with which I was connected, and enter the service of the Union ? That was before the various denominations had so generally arranged to conduct their Sunday-school work through denominational organizations. The influence and operations of the Union were then much more extensive than now, and no doubt, had I been inclined to enter into its service, it would have been very much, pecuniarily, to my advantage. But my prompt and decisive reply was that no pecuniary or any other inducement would lead me to leave my present position, so long as the Society desired my services. And so that question was settled.

CHAPTER XIII.

IN 1842 I made a journey west as far as Indianapolis
and St. Louis, in company with my brother-in-law,
Judge Barton, and my brother Talbut, who was a physician
in Indianapolis. Two or three incidents of the journey
may be here recorded.

One Sabbath was spent in Marietta, Ohio, where this
brother graduated at the college in that city. The day
was made busy in preaching and addresses connected with
my Sabbath-school work.

On our way down the Ohio River one day, in a thunder-
shower, my brother requested me to remind him on reaching Cincinnati to reveal a secret to me. That secret was,
as I learned on reaching the city, that we were then sitting
directly over several casks, not of whiskey but of *gun-
powder!* He was acquainted with some of the officials of
the steamer, and though it was unlawful to carry that article on the boat, they had told him of the fact. When
asked why he had seated himself in such a dangerous
place, his reply was that "if the boat should be struck
by lightning, or if for any cause the powder should be
exploded, we were probably as safe there as we should
be in any part of the steamer."

While in Cincinnati we visited the Lane Seminary. By
invitation of my brother, one evening, we attended a panorama of the infernal regions. My brother repeatedly
warned me against being frightened at what might be
seen. I will not describe the scenes there represented —

the chains of darkness, the gnashing of teeth, the unquenchable fire, etc. Suffice it to say they were awful, but not more so than what is revealed to us in the language of the Bible of the woes of the lost. But I think the descriptions in the Word of God much more likely to lead men to flee from the wrath to come, than any such mechanical representation. If we will not hear Moses and the prophets, neither would we be persuaded, though one should rise from the dead. This panorama, however, was merely a pecuniary not a religious affair.

We spent a Sabbath at Indianapolis. Every church in the city, except one small Baptist church, including that of our brother-in-law, Rev. Henry Ward Beecher, who was absent, was closed, that all the people might attend a camp-meeting in the outskirts of the city. The evening service was almost as much a pandemonium, so far as noise and confusion were concerned, as the one represented in the panorama we witnessed at Cincinnati. There was praying, half a dozen at a time, singing, shouting, exhortation, falling into a trance, etc. etc. Two or three of Mr. Beecher's young brothers were there. When a woman, with a shriek, fell into a trance, and was taken up by several of the brethren and carried into a tent, the Beechers hurried away and followed to see the result. They overheard the victim in the trance, and who, of course, was all unconscious, say : —

"Lay me down carefully, brothers!"

When at Chicago we found a young city with a population of sixteen thousand. We felt that we could stand in the center and almost shake the city. Its growth since then is one of the marvels of the age — now a city of probably over seven hundred thousand inhabitants.

One of the great inconveniences of our journey was the

mode of traveling. Then, of course, there were no rail-roads, and through much of the rich prairie-land our high-ways were corduroy roads, — timbers laid crosswise, — over which the stages or great lumber wagons went jolting, jolting, almost taking away one's breath, and requiring the utmost effort to keep the seat. One day our lumber wagon was filled up with mail-bags, among which we found our seats as best we could. The kind-hearted driver, seeing our inconvenience, consoled us with the statement that a new stage was to be put on the road in a few weeks. That was doubtless better for future travelers, but somehow very little consolation or comfort did it afford us, tired and bruised wayfarers as we were.

Another inconvenience we found was in our food. An Irishman fellow-traveler said : " I can't ate their cookin' out here." A very little could we eat, except at Indianap-olis and St. Louis, where we were entertained by New England friends. Almost every thing that was cooked was done in lard. Chicken fixings, ham even, and every thing else were made to swim in lard.

At St. Louis we found a real New England home for a few days with my oldest brother, Rev. Artemas Bullard, D.D., pastor of the First Presbyterian Church, which office he held with remarkable success for eighteen years, when he lost his life, with some thirty other citizens of St. Louis, in that fearful railroad accident at the Gasconade Bridge, in November, 1855.

On our return journey we took a steamer at Chicago, by way of the lakes, for Buffalo. When we found that we could not reach Buffalo before the Sabbath, though the captain on starting had assured us we could, we stopped over, on Saturday morning, at Mackinaw, or, as we used to call it in our geography lessons in my school days,

Michilimackinac. Here, with a New York clergyman, we conducted service forenoon and afternoon, at the old chapel of the American Board of Foreign Missions. This chapel was erected by the Board when it had a mission at the island many years before for the Indians. By stopping over for the Sabbath, we had an opportunity to look about this unique and romantic spot, and we also escaped a fearful gale upon the lake Sabbath night. The Great Western, that came in Monday morning, had a very rough time, and was much injured by the storm. But our sail to Buffalo on Monday was most delightful.

A Second Western Tour.

AT the end of twenty-five years' labor with the Society, in 1859 the Board gave me a vacation of ten weeks, to make a more extensive journey to the west for rest and recreation. Before starting I prepared the leading articles, with the engravings, for twelve numbers of *The Well-Spring.* These were put into the hands of the printer, and then I kept him supplied with all the copy he needed by my " Editorial Correspondence."

Mr. K. A. Burnell was then laboring as a missionary of the Society at the west. He was notified of my expected visit, and informed that I would be willing, now and then, to attend and address a meeting, if he wished to arrange for such services. On reaching him, I found that he had arranged for a meeting at two o'clock P. M. for children, and in the evening one for older persons, for every day for a week or two ! That, to be continued for a very long time, I felt would be rather over-doing the matter, inasmuch as it was a tour for rest.

I very soon found that the west was largely made up of New England people, and that most of them, in their younger days, were familiar with *The Well-Spring* or *The Sabbath-School Visitor*, and with the name of the editor; and every-where they were urgent for meetings. The Sabbaths at Detroit, Milwaukee, Chicago, Quincy, Lawrence in Kansas, St. Louis, Cincinnati, etc., were crowded with services.

At Chicago there were arranged three public meetings in different parts of the city; and I visited and addressed eight Sabbath-schools and the Bridewell.

At Milwaukee, besides several other services, there was a meeting in the afternoon of all the evangelical Sunday-schools of the city. It was held in the Spring Street Congregational Church, of which Rev. W. DeLoss Lane, D.D., now of South Hadley, Mass., was pastor.

After addressing the school of the Plymouth Church, which took a large number of *The Well-Spring*, the school, by a most hearty vote, sent greetings to their brothers and sisters of *The Well-Spring* family, and to the Sabbath-school children of New England.

I attended a Sabbath-school convention of several days, for southern Wisconsin, at Racine. At a mass meeting in a small grove, it was estimated that there were present four thousand children.

I also attended a large Sabbath-school convention at Fond du Lac, for northern Wisconsin. One evening meeting was addressed by Governor Randall and myself. The governor said he had been a scholar, teacher, and superintendent in the Sabbath-school. Though not a professor of religion, he expressed great interest in the cause.

In one of my addresses at a children's meeting, I had given expression to some fears lest his excellency might complain of my having entered his state without permission and stolen from him the hearts of the children. To this the governor replied : —

"If the reverend gentleman has stolen the hearts of the children of Wisconsin, he is welcome to them. It is the only thing he could have stolen and deserve to be pardoned; and I will pardon him freely without a petition. I do not think he will use the affection of the children for any bad purpose. In that case the end justifies the means."

My visit to Lawrence, Kansas, I had anticipated with much interest, as over $500 worth of Sunday-school books and papers had been sent by our Society to that city, to aid in promoting the Sabbath-school cause in Kansas. And these were the first publications of the kind sent to that territory. And besides, two Sabbath-schools had been organized in Lawrence by the names of Beecher and Bullard schools. At the close of my address, at a united meeting of the evangelical schools, at 4 o'clock P.M., by the suggestion of one of the superintendents, a collection was cheerfully taken to help meet the expenses of my western tour. This was also done at several meetings in different cities, without any suggestion from the speaker.

A somewhat curious occurrence took place in this city, showing the influence of the children compared with that of the women.

Notice had been given in the papers and by bulletins, without any intended opposition to our meeting, that the pastor of the Unitarian church would preach at four o'clock P.M. on Woman. That was the same hour at which our united meeting of the children was called. I said to the pastor of the Congregational church, Rev. Richard Cordley: "The women will beat the children and we shall have a small meeting. All will wish to hear what the preacher has to say about woman."

There was not as much said in public about woman as

at the present day. We went to our meeting, and to my surprise, the house was literally packed, every seat was occupied and many were standing.

While singing the hymn before the address we were still more surprised to see the Unitarian clergyman with all his congregation of *six women* come into our meeting. The children had carried the day.

My visit at St. Louis was especially noteworthy. This was only four years after the tragic death of my brother, the pastor of the First Presbyterian Church. A strong family resemblance secured for me every-where — in the street, in my many calls upon the families of this society, in the Sabbath-school, and in the church — an immediate recognition that was most affecting. While these scenes were a constant and almost painful appeal to all my tenderest emotions, they were still a most gratifying evidence of the deep affection with which the memory of my departed brother was cherished by his devoted people. There was scarcely any thing that touched my feelings more deeply than the tenderness with which the pastor, Rev. Dr. Nelson, frequently spoke of his predecessor, the sympathy he manifested with his people in their bereavement, and the pains he seemed to take to cherish among them these affectionate recollections of their departed friend. Had he been an own brother, I know not how he could have spoken of him with more esteem and love.

At the time of my visit to St. Louis in 1842 the population was about 32,000; at the time of this visit in 1859 it numbered not far from 190,000.

On the next Wednesday afternoon I addressed a large gathering of the Sabbath-schools of Indianapolis. This city is quite noted for its enterprise in the Sunday-school work. A few years before it was reported that nearly every child of the city that could be brought in was connected with some Sunday-school.

On Saturday, by special invitation of the Young Men's Christian Association of Cincinnati, I addressed a large children's meeting in a mammoth tent. In the morning of the Sabbath I addressed the school of the Presbyterian church that worshiped at the chapel of the Lane Theological Seminary on Walnut Hills. In the forenoon I preached at the Congregational church under the pastoral care of Rev. Henry M. Storrs. In the afternoon I addressed a mission school at the west end of the city, in their beautiful new chapel, and also a Methodist school. At three o'clock I addressed an interesting meeting of children and friends in Rev. Mr. Storrs' church, and in the evening preached to a great multitude at the tent.

This busy day closed the public labors of my western tour, and on Monday my steps were turned for home, which I safely reached on Friday morning, having been absent nine weeks and four days. In this tour I traveled about six thousand miles, preached and gave addresses ninety-eight times, and brought home to the Society one hundred dollars, more than the expenses of the tour.

On reaching home I found that the printer of *The Well-Spring* had not only received from me in my absence all the articles he needed for the paper, but enough for a month or two to come.

A Third Western Tour.

In the spring of 1864 the Sabbath-school in Grinnell, Iowa, through the teachers, several of whom were officers in the college in that place, invited me to visit the school at the time the Association of the state was to hold there its annual meeting. This school took a large number of

The Well-Spring, and the children, especially, wanted to see and hear the man who made it.

I commenced this tour May 27, 1864. The first day, in the western part of the state, the train narrowly escaped a fearful disaster. The engine displaced a short rail, hurling it several rods into the bushes. Two baggage cars were thrown from the track just as they were passing a deep culvert. The wheels of the forward one came within an inch or two of dropping into the culvert, by which event the whole train would have been instantly stopped, and no one can tell what a wreck would have been made by the concussion.

All spoke of our escape as wonderful, calling for the most devout thankfulness to a kind, superintending providence. I could but inquire, How many thought of the kind providence that had brought us all the way from Boston to that spot without any accident ?

In consequence of the detention caused by this disaster I spent the Sabbath at Lockport, N. Y., instead of Detroit, Mich., according to my plan. Rev. Joseph L. Bennett, pastor of the Congregational church, at once arranged for me to preach in the morning at the Methodist church; at noon to address the Sunday-school of that church and his own ; at three P.M. address a united meeting of five schools ; and in the evening preach at a united meeting of the Presbyterian and Methodist churches.

At Grinnell the Association, which commenced its session on Wednesday, was held through the week and on the Sabbath. At 1 o'clock P.M. on Saturday, the Association suspended its business and gave up the church for a meeting of the Sunday-schools in Grinnell and the adjacent towns, that the scholars might see and hear "the man who makes *The Well-Spring.*" I also had an opportunity of addressing the school that had invited me there on the Sabbath.

A little three-year-old boy came to the children's meeting, expecting to see something marvelous, as he had been told that "the man who makes" *The Well-Spring* was going to speak.   After looking some time at the speaker, he turned to his mother and said with an expression of sore disappointment : "Why, mother, he is only an old man!"   He was expecting to see some wonderful animal, such as he had once seen at a show or exhibition; but instead of that he was only an old man.   He little knew how young that old man's heart was.

On leaving Grinnell, I visited several towns and cities in Iowa, as far west as Des Moines, which is very near the center of our continent, and on my return journey I visited Cincinnati and Indianapolis.   Meetings were held in all these places.

In this tour of about one month, I traveled three thousand two hundred and eighty miles, visited thirteen towns and parishes, and preached or gave addresses thirty-three times.   My "Editorial Correspondence" for *The Well-Spring*, giving an account of the various places visited and the scenes and events witnessed, were published in fifteen consecutive numbers.

CHAPTER XIV.

SOME EXCURSIONS.

Visit to Prince Edward's Island.

THROUGH the courtesy of the late Frank Snow, Esq., of Boston, president of the Boston and Colonial Steamship Company, and Captain P. A. Nickerson, of the steamer Alhambra, I had a free passage to Prince Edward's Island in the summer of 1866. We touched at Halifax and Plaister Cove, and reached Charlottetown, the capital of the island, seven hundred miles from Boston, in seventy-two hours.

Sabbath morning there was a large fire that destroyed nearly $300,000 worth of property. This calamity deranged nearly all my plans for services in the churches and Sabbath-schools for that day.

The superintendent of the Wesleyan school, William Heard, Esq., learning that my accommodations at a public house were not altogether comfortable, most kindly invited me to his beautiful home, where for more than a week his interesting family gave me the most hospitable entertainment.

The next Sabbath I preached in the forenoon at the National Scotch Presbyterian Church; at half-past two addressed the Episcopal school, and at three o'clock addressed a united meeting of all the Protestant schools in the city, excepting the Wesleyan, which was preparing for a special meeting for the evening. This school, which numbered over four hundred, held its fiftieth anniversary in the evening.   The senior preacher, Dr. Richey, and the new young preacher, who that day began his work with that people, and also the superintendent of the school, all invited me to preach a Sabbath-school sermon on the occasion.   This invitation I most gladly accepted.   Although I was seeking to recruit my somewhat impaired health, this was too important an opportunity to do hopeful work, to be unimproved.   Every church in the city gave up its evening service to attend this fiftieth anniversary of a Sunday-school.

The spacious new chapel of this people was completely packed ; and the seats were arranged in a sort of amphitheater, so that the immense audience seemed closely around the speaker.   Never, before or since, have I spoken under the pressure of such an excitement.   For in no other instance had I felt while speaking the stimulus of the oft-repeated and emphatic "Amen ! " " That 's true ! " etc.

On Tuesday afternoon I was invited to a public gathering — or, as it is there called, " tea " — of this people in a pleasant grove, for a further commemoration of their interesting anniversary, and where another opportunity was given me for an address.

Through the kindness of several gentlemen I had five or six delightful drives and excursions into the country and across the island.   One of these was fourteen miles to the north side of the island, to a place called Rustico. After a pleasant sail in company with the rector of the Church of England and about twenty of his people, we had a fine picnic, spreading a table-cloth on the ground, and seating ourselves in rustic style on the grass.

I returned to Halifax by steamer to Glasgow, and then across Nova Scotia, forty-one miles by stage and sixty by rail. At New Glasgow, with a friend I had met on a boat, I went two miles to visit the Albion coal-mines. With a guide we went half a mile into one of these mines, till we came to the shaft where the coal is drawn up. We were, perhaps, a hundred or a hundred and fifty feet from the surface. The passage where the coal had been taken out was from ten to twenty feet wide and ten or twelve feet high. Every once in awhile we came to a large passage, running out on one side or the other, far into total darkness, showing what vast quantities of coal had been taken out. And then, on either side of us and overhead, it was all coal, no one knows how thick.

When we reached the shaft, we were told that the men were at work blasting out the coal "a mile farther in"! But we did not care to pursue our way, with only two little lights, any further into this deep darkness.

Close by the shaft there were extensive stables for the horses, dug out of the solid mass of coal. There were the hostler and two or three boys, with small lamps fastened to the front of their caps, who have the care of the horses. The horses are employed in drawing cars, or small boxes of coal, on a railway to the shaft, where they are drawn up by machinery and emptied. The horses never leave the mines to see the light of day till they are disabled.

When at Halifax I visited the gold-mines at Waverley, sixteen miles from the city. There were five or six companies successfully working the mines. Some of the mines had been worked down one hundred or two hundred feet. The crushers by which the gold-bearing quartz is reduced to fine dust consist of from six to sixteen steel or iron upright shafts, each weighing six hundred pounds. A horizontal shaft runs near the top of these, with a flange for each. This is turned by steam-power, causing these heavy shafts to rise at irregular times and fall upon dies at the bottom, crushing or pounding to dust the quartz, as it is shoveled in large lumps into the hopper. A stream of water is constantly flowing in upon this, washing it, as it becomes fine, through a sieve, carrying away the stone-dust and leaving the fine gold, which is heavier, to settle into little cups, where it mingles with quicksilver and forms an amalgam. This is put into a retort, and by means of heat the mercury is passed off in a vapor and condensed for use again, and the fine gold is left. It is a very curious and interesting process.

On the Sabbath at Halifax, I held several services and, among others, addressed a united meeting of the various schools in the city.

On Tuesday evening I had the pleasure of attending a quarterly meeting of the Halifax and Dartmouth Sunday-school Association, which embraces fourteen schools connected with the different evangelical churches. This gave me the opportunity of seeing and addressing a large number of the teachers in that region.

In this visit of twenty-four days I traveled fourteen hundred miles and preached and gave addresses eleven times.

The " Coit Excursionists "

WAS an organization composed of citizens of Worcester and vicinity for an annual steamboat excursion. It took its name from the captain of the steamer in which the company of two or three hundred made their first excursion. In 1870 I was permitted to accompany the members of this association, in the fine steamer New Brunswick, Captain S. H. Pike, in an excursion to the principal towns along the coast of Maine, to St. John and Fredericton, the capital of the Province.

On this excursion I was often called on to aid the chaplain in the religious and social services of his office. This was an occasion of much-needed relief from my daily round of duties. The company was select and the social intercourse very enjoyable.

In 1871 the

Bay State Excursion

was projected. On the eighth of August a company of two hundred and fifty started from Commercial Wharf, Boston, in the above-named steamer, for an eight days' excursion on the eastern coast. This excursion extended to St. John and Fredericton.

The company, soon after getting under way, was formally organized by the choice of officers — president, vice-presidents, secretary, chaplain, surgeon, and executive committee. I was chosen president and chaplain. As the company was divided, for convenience' sake, into two sections for dinner, one section receiving their meals first one day and the other the next, and the chaplain was called on to officiate at each, and as the president and executive committee had to make all the arrangements for the evening entertainments, and the president had to preside at all the meetings held with the citizens of the various towns and cities visited, this excursion, while it was in all respects very pleasant, was to me a very busy one.

Mr. C. B. Tillinghast, the secretary, prepared and published an interesting and very sprightly account of this tour in a handsome little volume of 69 pages, called " The Bay State Excursion of 1871." The following extract may be given here : —

At a farewell meeting on our return, in Portland harbor, a sub-committee on resolutions, appointed by the executive committee, reported, among quite a number of others, the following preamble and resolution : —

" The kind-hearted president and chaplain, Rev. Asa Bullard, who devotedly administered to the spiritual 'needs of the excursionists, and whose uniform courtesy won for him from every heart the deepest feelings of respect and regard, was remembered in the following resolution, which was unanimously adopted : —

" *Resolved*, That the Rev. Asa Bullard, in double capacity of chaplain and president, by his indefatigable, constant, and unceasing labor in our behalf, has greatly contributed to our happiness, and that we tender to him our heartfelt thanks. Always hereafter, until the pulse of life shall cease to beat, we will recall with gratitude and pleasure the very successful manner in which he has acquitted himself as our spiritual guide over the beautiful waters and along the rock-bound, evergreen shores of Maine and New Brunswick, as well as towards those as yet unseen but forever unclouded shores, where the wicked cease from troubling and the weary are at rest.

" We will fondly treasure his memory upon earth, and cherish the hope that we may all meet him, at the end of life's short voyage, in heaven."

Mr. Bullard responded to this resolution with much feeling and with words that touched the hearts of all.

A year or two afterwards there was another Bay State Excursion ; but some trouble in securing a suitable steamer, together with some other circumstances, made that occasion less satisfactory than the former one.

Massachusetts Press Association.

For several years I was connected with the Massachusetts Press Association. A large portion of the editors and publishers of the state were connected with the association. Every year this society had an excursion, in various directions, of two or three weeks for rest and recreation.

It would be difficult to bring together a more genial and in all respects interesting company of traveling companions. All but the officers who had the arrangement for the excursions, and especially the treasurer, who had all the bills to settle, etc., were entirely at their leisure and could enjoy all the changing scenes through which they passed. I had the great pleasure of joining in several of these excursions. One year the association visited the great international exhibition at Philadelphia. The tickets entitled the members, with their ladies, to the journey there and back and to entertainments and free access to all parts of the exhibition while there.

Another excursion took us to Saratoga, St. George, across Lake Champlain to Burlington, Vt., where we had our re-union exercises in the evening.

Still another memorable excursion was to Montreal, Quebec, and up the Saguenay River. We spent a Sabbath at Quebec, where I had an opportunity for abundant labor in connection with the churches and the Sunday-schools. The same was true wherever we spent the Sabbath in any of the excursions referred to. As I was usually the only clergyman on these excursions of the press association, I was made the chaplain of the occasion.

CHAPTER XV.

MY VISIT ABROAD.

THERE is, perhaps, no one privilege connected with my temporal happiness that I have prized more highly or that has afforded me more true enjoyment than my three months' visit abroad in 1880; and I am most happy to acknowledge my indebtedness for this privilege to my late beloved pastor, Rev. James S. Hoyt, D.D., now of Keokuk, Iowa.

Entirely unknown to me, he obtained from some of my Sabbath-school friends and some of our Sabbath-schools the means of my going as a delegate to the centenary of Sunday-schools in London.

Dr. Hoyt's first plan was to obtain the means for me only to attend this meeting and return. But the responses to his letters were so liberal that he was able one Friday evening at the close of our weekly prayer-meeting, to the surprise of every one, to present me with a five hundred dollar excursion ticket for a tour in Europe for three months. The applause of the people present was most unbounded. He then informed those present that I should be likely to need a little money in my pocket; and, as the ticket was obtained outside of his own congregation, many of the church and society and the Sabbath-school most generously met this need. The Board of our Society kindly gave me the necessary vacation for this visit, allowed my salary to continue, and added a grant of money, and the occupants of the Congregational House added their generous gifts; so that I was able easily to meet all the expenses of the tour.

On the twelfth of June, at eight o'clock in the morning, I left New York on board the Anchoria. Sabbath forenoon I had the privilege of preaching on the steamer to a large and appreciative audience.

All the forenoon it was very foggy, and the steam whistle was constantly giving forth its shrill, warning notes several times a minute. At one o'clock we lunched, after which two or three of us were still at the table making arrangements for a Bible service in the afternoon, when we were run into by the steamer Queen. Our boat sunk two feet almost instantly. The cry was given : —

" All on deck ! Lower the boats ! Women and children get in first ! "

I was the last passenger off the boat. We all were taken aboard the Queen, the bows of which were all stove in, but it was not injured as much as the Anchoria. What was singular is that if our boat had been twenty-five minutes farther ahead or the Queen had been twenty-five minutes later we should have been in clear sunshine. The Queen came out of clear weather into a bank of fog, coming upon us as a great phantom. It could not be seen the length of the boat. Both boats had compartments, or both would have sunk instantly. Two compartments of the Anchoria filled with water at once.

As it was calm weather, the two boats made their way slowly to New York, taking two days to sail three hundred miles.

On Thursday we sailed again on the Ethiopia, and had a most delightful voyage. Some thought it would be tempting providence for us to start again ; but it seemed to me that it would be distrusting providence not to go.

Fearing it might be foggy on the Sound, I took the steamer Narragansett for New York one night earlier than I otherwise should, and that was the night before she was burned! Had I waited till the next night, I should have been aboard the Stonington, that ran into the ill-fated Narragansett, and should have been too late for my steamer. Having passed safely through these two perils, under a kind providence, why should I not trust him in the future?

On account of our delay we did not reach Glasgow till Monday morning, the twenty-eighth, the day when, at twelve o'clock noon, the great Sunday-school convention was to be organized. So I left the party with which I was to visit in Scotland, before the meeting, and went four hundred miles, fifty miles an hour, reaching London in the evening. The next morning I went to the convention and attended the meetings through the week. On Tuesday, the next week, I returned, four hundred miles, back to Glasgow, to meet the party that left New York on the twenty-sixth, and with which I was to travel on the Continent. I might have waited in London till the party came, but I could not give up old Scotland, of which I had heard so much all my life, of its regard for the Bible and the Sabbath, the wise family government and training.

Our tour was through some of the most noted places in Scotland, England, Holland, on to Berlin, Dresden, Leipsic, Prague, Vienna, over the Semmering Pass to Adlerberg, into the stalactite cavern seven miles, to Trieste, Venice, Milan, Verona, upon the beautiful lakes of northern Italy, through all the important cities of Switzerland to Paris, and back to London and home.

The whole tour was one of great enjoyment. My health was never better; and this visit abroad has been a source of joy to me, almost daily, ever since. Some account of it that I gave, after our return, in *The Congregationalist*, may appropriately be repeated here : —

My many friends who so kindly interested themselves in my late visit to Europe may expect some public account of it. In a tour of three months, in company with thirty or forty persons, mostly strangers to each other, and of various tastes and temperaments, as may be supposed, there will be many little inconveniences and things to annoy ; and it would be the easiest thing in the world for one to make himself delightfully miserable by allowing himself to be constantly disturbed by them.

In one of the gloomy cells of the London Tower, the walls are covered with incriptions sculptured by those who have there suffered confinement. Among these are the following : " Grief is overcome by patience. G. Gryfford, August 8th, 1586." " The most unhappy man in the world is he that is not patient in adversities. For men are not killed with the adversities they have, but with ye impatience which they suffer." This is signed : " Charles Bailey. Æt. 29. 10 Sept., 1571." And yet this Charles Bailey was an adherent of Mary Queen of Scots, and suffered the tortures of the rack without making any disclosures of importance.

Foreseeing the little vexations likely to occur in connection with the anticipated tour, it was my deliberate resolve, in entering upon it, to " possess my soul in patience" in all circumstances, and get all the enjoyment possible out of it. While this resolve was, to a good degree, carried out, it must be acknowledged that there were abundant opportunites for " patience to have its perfect work." There were a few, especially of the more amiable sex, who seemed to see something for their discomfort at nearly every step, and they very freely expressed it. Complaining and fretting at something or other was the constant burden of their song. And to many of the party this was certainly a burden if not a song.

Some may wish to know the advantages or disadvantages of making such a tour with an excursion party. For most persons, especially ladies, going alone, or unattended by any who have been before, an excursion party, with all the little inconveniences attending it, — particularly if the courier be intelligent, courteous, and gentlemanly, — has many advantages. The party need have no care for their baggage, for securing rooms at the hotels, paying bills for board and service, fees for guides, for making arrangements for carriages and seats together in the cars, obtaining railroad tickets and tickets for concerts, cathedrals, palaces, picture galleries, etc., or selecting the important cities and objects in these cities to be visited. All this is the proper duty of the courier, and it takes a great deal of care from the visitors, and prevents much waste of time. Then there are some places of special interest to which individuals would scarcely gain admittance. The managers of these excursions secure this privilege for large parties beforehand.

There are also pleasant acquaintances formed in such a party. Not infrequently among the younger members not a little innocent flirtation is observed. Sometimes this develops into permanent attachments, and sometimes they end with the excursion. Single ladies have been encouraged to join these parties with the assurance that soon they would find themselves quite at home. The chief danger in such cases is that they may seek to attach themselves to one or more, as their companions at the table and in the frequent walks and rides of the party, without carefully ascertaining whether such companionship is mutually agreeable. In such a company there will inevitably be a grouping together in little clans of those of similar tastes and feeling. And then again some may prefer becoming acquainted with most or all of the party, and it may be annoying to have some particular one watching for his or her company at every turn.

A member of a late European party said she wished there were more gentlemen, it was so handy to have them about to carry your bag for you. Most gentlemen have their own hand-baggage to look after; and then it may be supposed they have some other objects in view than to look after the luggage of ladies who travel alone.

It is my decided conviction that, as this was my first visit abroad, it was best that it should be made as it was, with an excursion party, unless it could have been in company of one or two who had been before. While there were some things not so agreeable, over which it would have been easy to have made myself unhappy, yet, it is due to my friends to say, all things considered, that the tour was most enjoyable, and one of the happiest three months of my life.

The great objection to these excursions is that, while you may be able to visit many more places in the same time, these visits are too hurried. You go as a pilgrim and tarry, as it were, but for a night. You have no time to learn any thing of the people, their manners and customs and home life, except what you can see while flying through one city after another.

A second visit, in company with two or three friends, would most surely, in my judgment, be much more satisfactory and profitable, made independently; and it would probably be at quite as small expense. Let the route be carefully laid out before starting; then secure rooms by letter or telegraph a few days or weeks in advance, and then remain at each place as long as you may find it desirable. Such a visit I should be most happy to make, should a kind providence ever open the way.

It is well known that generally throughout Europe the Sabbath is not observed as it is with us. It is a holiday. Shops are open, and traffic of all sorts is carried on much as on other days. Parades and shows are even more frequent on Sunday than any other day of the week. There is great temptation, even for those who are accustomed to observe the Sabbath and attend public worship at home, to fall into the habits of the people around them when abroad. In many of the European cities there are places of Protestant worship, designed especially for the benefit of tourists and the English-speaking residents, but there are comparatively few who attend them. In too many instances even professing Christian tourists spend their Sabbaths much as they do the other days of the week.

At the Sunday-school Centenary in London, one speaker said some one asked a boy if his father was a Christian. "Yes," said he, "he is a Christian, but he doesn't do much at it." It is to be feared that there are not a few professing Christians who do not do much at their profession when abroad. If a cooper or a blacksmith or a merchant should do as little at his profession, he would find himself on the way to the almshouse.

It was my purpose in starting on my late European tour to take my religion, so far as I had any, along with me; to do nothing on the Sabbath or any other day that would be inconsistent with my Christian profession at home; so that the comforts and hopes of religion might be my support in times of prosperity or of peril. The first Sabbath on the continent was spent in Berlin. Divine service was held in the forenoon in the American chapel. This service is conducted by theological students, mostly from this country, who are pursuing their theological studies in that city. This is the only place where Protestant worship is held in the city; and this is maintained, as in several other cities, for the special benefit of English and American residents and tourists. Many of our party, and not a few of them professing Christians, instead of attending this service, both for their own spiritual good and the encouragement of those by whom it is maintained, took an excursion of fifteen miles to Potsdam, the Versailles of Prussia, and spent the day in visiting its splendid palaces, works, museums, and other objects of interest. A Sabbath was passed in Vienna and also in Venice, but there were no English or American services. In the latter, I went in the morning to attend high mass at St. Mark's, but was too late; and the afternoon service was all in an unknown tongue, and the bowings and courtesying and burning of incense seemed so unchristian that I sought a sanctuary in my own room.

At Bellagio, on Lake Como, there was an English church near our hotel; but, as a clergyman of our party, whose habits had greatly damaged his character as a minister and a Christian in the eyes of most of those who had been in his company, was expected to take part in the service, very few attended. Some thought they could worship more to their taste under the great dome of the skies, amid the grand and picturesque scenes of lake and mountain around them; and others found their Bethel in the quietness of their own rooms. Among other religious reading I found Paul's Epistle to the Hebrews most stimulating and instructive; and I would commend it to all tourists as very excellent and profitable reading for the Sabbath day.

At Lucerne several of the party attended service in the forenoon and evening in a Catholic church, and heard two instructive sermons by a Scotch Presbyterian minister. The city authorities have placed this church at the service of the Protestants for these two services, when the Catholics do not use it. Although the walls of the church were hung with pictures and images of the saints, and a light was visible through the screen before the altar, yet the voice of praise and prayer and the proclamation of the good news of salvation through a Redeemer were sweet and refreshing.

At Geneva, Rev. Dr. Stevens, formerly editor of *Zion's Herald* in Boston, is maintaining religious services in the little American chapel where Rev. Leonard W. Bacon, D.D., now of Norwich, Conn., for some years preached. A young minister preached an excellent sermon, appropriate to tourists, on the words: "We have here no continuing city." I had the pleasure of addressing the little Sabbath-school before the service, and of participating in the exercises of the evening meeting for prayer and conference.

Our last Sabbath in Europe was in Paris. Rev. Dr. Hitchcock preached in the morning. I attended his Sabbath-school, which he invited me to address. He, in connection with a band of earnest missionary laborers, is doing a good work in this city of pleasure and worldliness. The money, in part, has been collected for a new and commodious church, in place of the chapel which so many friends and Sabbath-schools in America, some years ago, so generously aided in building.

On our return voyage it was too rough and boisterous for a morning service the first Sabbath, but Rev. Dr. Lang, of Glasgow, pastor of the church where the late Dr. MacLeod used to speak, in the evening spoke on the words : " When thou passest through the waters, I will be with thee." His words were most comforting, as so many had been awe-stricken when " no small tempest lay on us."

Several days, when the weather would permit, a season of family worship was held, and a meeting for prayer and addresses on Wednesday evening, when so many of the churches at home were holding their usual weekly meeting ; and also on the evening of our last Sabbath, Rev. Dr. Lang preached a most eloquent and practical sermon in the morning, on the words : " The grace of the Lord Jesus Christ, and the love of God, and the communion of the Holy Ghost be with you all."

It seems to me that I have had more enjoyment in every thing adapted to impart joy from my attempt to maintain the same Christian life while abroad, on the Sabbath and every day, as when at home.

The Sunday-School Centenary.

ALL who may be interested in reading this volume may be glad to see a brief account of the great international convention in London, commemorative of the founding of Sabbath-schools by Robert Raikes.

This convention was planned and admirably conducted by the London Sunday-School Union. It commenced on Monday, the twenty-eighth of June, at noon, and continued through the week.

Saturday evening, the twenty-sixth, the Union gave a reception to the foreign delegates, at their rooms, 56 Old Bailey, directly opposite the old Newgate Prison of London. This meeting was one of great interest. There

were present at the convention about three hundred
foreign delegates from Belgium, Holland, Sweden, Germany, Austria, Italy, Switzerland, and France, on the
continent ; one or two, even, from Australia, fifteen or
sixteen thousand miles distant ; Pastor Jacob and his
wife, from Oroomiah, Persia, and others from Canada
and the United States. A large portion of these delegates were from America. The whole number, including
those in Great Britain, was nearly a thousand.

After a formal reception of the delegates by Sir
Thomas Chambers, President of the Union, and Sir
Charles Reed, one of its officials, addresses were made
by Messrs. Reed and Higgs of Gloucester; Dr. Vincent,
of New York ; Vice-Chancellor Blake, President of the
Sunday-School Union of Canada ; Mr. Woodruff, of New
York ; Pastors Paul Cook and H. Taumier, of Paris ;
Mr. H. G. Wade, Secretary of Victoria Sunday-School
Union in Australia ; Mr. John Wanamaker, of Philadel-
phia ; Pastor Truve, D.D., President of the Sunday-School
Union of Sweden ; M. P. Palenquist, the Robert Raikes
of Sweden ; Dr. Burns, of Nova Scotia ; M. Brockel-
mann, Sunday-school missionary for Germany, and Dr.
Lowrie, of New Jersey, the author of "Shall we gather
at the river?"

This meeting was a fine introduction for the meetings
of the coming convention.

On Sunday there were several large and spirited meetings of the children of the Sabbath-schools, in different
sections of the city.

The meeting for organization was at twelve o'clock on
Monday, at Guild Hall, and was presided over by the
Right Honorable the Lord Mayor. In his introductory
address he said : "To my mind nothing can be more
appropriate than that the centenary of Robert Raikes'

great work, the Sunday-school movement, should be commemorated in the grand old Guild Hall of the city of London." Addresses were also made by the Archbishop of Canterbury, Dr. Vincent, Lord Hatherly, Alderman McArthur, M.P., since then chosen Lord Mayor of London, and several others.

The subjects on which papers were read and addresses made during the week, by persons previously appointed, were the following: "The past history of the Sunday-school system;" "Position and prospects of Sunday-schools on the Continent of Europe;" "The Church of Christ, in its relations to Sunday-school work;" "The Word of God the appointed instrument of religious education;" "An efficient Sunday-school agency: its nature and the means of its attainment;" and "The future of the Sunday-school system."

These various topics were well presented in thoroughly prepared papers, though some of them were quite too long, and by studied and earnest addresses. There was very little opportunity for a free discussion by the delegates generally on any of the subjects before the convention. The prominent Sabbath-school men from the United States, Drs. Taylor, Hall, and Vincent, and others from New York; Mr. Woodruff, of Brooklyn; Messrs. Wanamaker, of Philadelphia, and Jacobs, of Chicago, and a few others, had a due share in the exercises, and no speakers acquitted themselves more acceptably to those addressed.

Tuesday evening there were four meetings in different parts of the city, for popular addresses on various branches of the Sabbath-school work. These services were especially practical and stimulating.

As the Sabbath-school work is comparatively new in most places on the continent, most of the schools having been established within the past twelve or fifteen years, the reports and remarks of the delegates from those sections were much like those we used to hear in our own country, twenty-five or thirty years ago. There was much zeal and earnestness in their manner and words, but not very much that was new to those who had been in the work a quarter or half a century.

Perhaps the most enthusiastic and stimulating meeting was on Thursday evening, at Exeter Hall, and four of the speakers were from our own country.

The children's day was on Wednesday. Forty-six thousand persons gathered at the world-renowned Crystal Palace, at Sydenham, fifteen miles from the city. All the exercises had special reference to the children, and were attended with extraordinary attractions. There was a grand concert, in which five thousand well-trained children delighted an immense audience for an hour. After this there was a mass concert upon the terraces of the palace, in which thirty thousand united their voices with bands of instrumental music.

A delightful surprise was occasioned by the letting on of the water to the numerous fountains, which was thrown up in most fantastic forms. And there were games and athletic sports for the children, with prizes, and a balloon ascension, and many other arrangements, all for the gratification of the young. In all the services of this occasion, and in this great gathering of men, women, and children, there was not a single case of disorderly conduct or of intoxication. That Wednesday must long remain in the memory of all those who were present as a day of remarkable interest. That fairy palace, too, made wholly of iron and glass, sixteen hundred feet long and three hundred feet wide, with its beautiful grounds, must have been photographed on the minds of all.

On Saturday the beautiful and appropriate bronze statue of Robert Raikes was unveiled by Lord Shaftsbury, in the Victoria Garden, on the Embankment, in the presence of a large audience. It is almost directly opposite Cleopatra's Needle, where for ages it may be seen by the myriads who will pass and re-pass on that frequented and delightful promenade.

But the scene in connection with this centenary that most deeply moved the feelings of every Christian heart was the communion service at the Metropolitan Tabernacle. Mr. Spurgeon, the pastor of that church, presided, and made a most tender and touching address. There were between four and five thousand communicants present. At the close, by the request of Mr. Spurgeon, all that immense audience joined hands and sang Cowper's hymn : —

"Ere since by faith I saw the stream," etc.

That scene alone was worth all it cost of money and time and fatigue and peril to cross and re-cross the ocean. I never expect again to see the like on earth.

Before commencing this visit abroad, I prepared the leading articles, with the illustrations, of sixteen numbers of *The Well-Spring.* I prepared three articles on the steamer each way, and a large number while in Europe, which were sent to the printer. We reached home on Monday, and on Tuesday copy was wanted for the seventeenth number.

For many weeks after my return accounts of the places I visited and the scenes I witnessed were published in *The Well-Spring.* Those articles might interest the readers of this volume, but they would swell it to an unreasonable size.

CHAPTER XVI.

THE CHESTNUT STORY.

NO proper sketch of my life in connection with the Sabbath-school could be given, that did not include my "chestnut story." It is one of the most remarkable Sunday-school stories of the age.

Perhaps I can not better present it here than in the familiar and informal way in which I used to repeat it in some of my addresses at Sabbath-school meetings, when speaking on the subject of doing good.

Rev. George Constantine, D.D., now of Bombay, was born in Athens, Greece. He was converted to Protestantism by our foreign missionary, the late Rev. Dr. King. He came to this country, and while at the high school in Cambridge was converted to Christ. He then went to Amherst College in 1855.

He soon heard of a neighborhood, about four miles from college and within the same distance from twelve evangelical churches, where four towns come together: Shutesbury, Leverett, Pelham, and Amherst, and which was often called "the devil's corner." No one seemed to be taking any concern about the spiritual interest of this neglected neighborhood.

Mr. Constantine said to himself: "That is no missionary spirit at all, that sends missionaries to Greece and Africa and heathen lands, and leaves a people within four miles of twelve evangelical churches uncared for!"

So he went to that neighborhood and established a Sabbath-school; and every Sabbath, at four o'clock in the afternoon, he walked four miles and conducted it. So George Constantine, of Greece, became a foreign missionary in old Puritan Massachusetts!

I spent a Sabbath in Leverett, and at four o'clock in the afternoon visited and addressed Mr. Constantine's mission Sunday-school. After my visit, some of the children wanted to take a collection to send books and papers to poor children at the west. Mr. Constantine told them if they did they must earn or save the money they were to give.

So the children went to work. The boys picked stones, packed shingles, went on errands, picked nuts, etc. One boy — whom they called "deacon" because he brought in all the new scholars, and who left off his hat and shoes because "them other boys did n't wear none, and they would feel badly if he did" — picked four quarts of walnuts. The girls helped their mothers in various ways. One little girl sewed six weeks and her mother gave her a cent! Was n't that good wages?

Mrs. Nurse, a poor woman, picked two quarts of chestnuts and sold them to get money for her contribution. Some family wants led her to use the money, intending to pick some more chestnuts for the contribution. One cold afternoon she took a neighbor's little girl and went in search of chestnuts. There were not many that season, and the squirrels had gathered what there were. After searching some time and finding none, they came to a tree where the ground was covered with leaves. They got down upon their knees and began to brush away the leaves, when they came upon a little heap of about half a pint of chestnuts, that a squirrel, perhaps, had gathered for winter's use, and forgotten where he hid them.

When the contribution day came Mrs. Nurse was n't

present.   After school Mr. Constantine called on her and found her looking very sad.   In answer to his inquiry why she was not at school, she said : —

"I had n't any thing to give, and I did n't want to go."

She then told him about her using the money she meant to have given, but she had nothing now only these few chestnuts.

"Well," said Mr. Constantine, "perhaps I will take your chestnuts."

"Will you ?" she anxiously inquired ; "I think God will bless them, for I wanted to give something."

As the result of the contribution of this school to the Society, I received three hundred cents, four quarts of walnuts, and half a pint of chestnuts.   For the walnuts I gave twenty-five cents a quart, when I could have purchased ever so many for half that price.   So I paid into the treasury of our Society, as a donation from this school, $4.00.   I now had left on hand the chestnuts, for which I hoped in some way to obtain fifty cents or a dollar, and send word to the donor that "God had blessed her offering."

New Year's night I was invited to attend a gathering and supper of the Sabbath-school at Winchester, Mass. I said : "I will take the chestnuts and see what can be done with them."   I counted them over, and found one hundred and fifty that were sound and good, though all of them were very small.   There were very few that year and they could n't afford to grow very large.

In the course of my address at the gathering, I related the story of the chestnuts, and held up the bag containing them, and said : "The good woman thinks God will bless them ; now what shall we do with them ? Friends, what shall we do with these chestnuts ?"

A teacher said : " Why not put them up at auction ? "

" Very well," I replied ; " we will, if you will act as auctioneer ; " and he was an auctioneer.

They were soon bid off for five dollars. The man who bought them put them up again, and they were bid off for two dollars and fifty cents.

I supposed this was the last of it. God *had* blessed them, and I could inform the good woman that they had been sold for seven dollars and fifty cents, and the money given to the Society to aid in establishing Sunday-schools at the west.

It was stormy at the time of this meeting, and the attendance was so small that the meeting was adjourned one week, and I was invited to be present.

In the meantime the auctioneer obtained possession of the chestnuts, and divided them into four little bags. In the course of the meeting he related the story of the chestnuts and said he was going to put them up at auction again. " But," said he," since the last meeting chestnuts is riz', so I can't sell them all at once. I shall sell them one bag at a time."

They were then bid off for two dollars and fifty cents a bag — in all, ten dollars, or, including the former sale, seventeen dollars and fifty cents. I bought one bag to keep, to remember the giver. Two of the purchasers gave me their bags, saying, " Perhaps you can turn them to further account."

Soon after this I attended a Sabbath-school meeting at the Congregational church at East Cambridge (that house of worship has since been removed to West Somerville). I carried my three bags of chestnuts with me and, in the course of my address, told the story of the chestnuts, held up my little bags, and informed the audience as to their great value, and that I could not sell for less than about five dollars a bag. In a few days a little boy of that school called on me and said with great enthusiasm : —

"Mr. Bullard, our school has raised five dollars, and I want to get one of your bags of chestnuts to give to our superintendent!"

The next week another little boy came, saying in the same excited manner : —

"Mr. Bullard, our school has raised five dollars more, to buy the bag of chestnuts away from our superintendent and give it to our minister!"

And soon after, the minister gave me the bag to sell again for the Sabbath-school cause.

A little after this the superintendent of that school suggested that I should get some of those wonderful chest-nuts blown into little glass bottles by the Bohemian Glass Blowers, who were then in his neighborhood. Accordingly I had, in all, perhaps one hundred and twenty-five of them blown into these little decanters, or bottles with curious stoppers in variegated colors. A part of the fourth bag at length came into my hands, so that I had about one hundred and thirty.

These little bottles were sold in every direction, for from five to ten dollars apiece. Many of them were sent back to me to be sold over again.

In my visit to the west in 1859, I took several of them and left them in every state I visited, as far west as Kansas for which I obtained about one hundred and thirty dollars.

One of the most remarkable cases was at the Sabbath school of the Phillips Church, South Boston, of which Rev. Dr. E. K. Alden, now of the American Board, was then pastor. The superintendent requested me to relate the "chestnut story." After school he asked me to leave one of the bottles, as he thought they could do something with it. The school went to taking up collections till they had raised thirty dollars, which they thought was a fair sum for it. Under the interest thus excited, they went to taking collections to clothe poor children, in which they raised quite a little sum. Then the school presented the chestnut to their minister, and he soon sent to the Society ten dollars to constitute the chestnut a life member of the Society.

In relating the story to the Sabbath-school children, I frequently referred to the fact that the stopper was blown in, and that I wished all decanters and bottles had the stoppers blown in. It would help in the temperance work. "Now," I would say, "you see, you can not get this stopper out, except in the way the little boy got the money out of his money-pot, as he called it.

" 'Mother,' " said he, 'I wish I had a cent.'

" 'What do you want a cent for, my boy?'

" 'I want to buy a money-pot,'

"It was a little porcelain mug with a slit in the top through which to slip in money, a sort of bank or contribution box, which the boy wanted. He got his money-pot and showed it to his uncle, who said : —

" 'What is that?'

" 'Uncle,' said he, 'won't you slip a twenty-five cent piece in there, and see how it will ring?'

"His uncle slipped in the money, but he could n't get it out again.

"One day some time after, the little boy came to his mother and said : —

" 'Mother, my money-pot is very heavy. and I wish I knew how much money is in it. If you will roll out the table and put on the table-cloth, I will get a hammer and hit the money-pot a crack, and we will see how much money there is.'"

So his mother prepared the table and the little boy hit his money-pot a crack, and out came — how much? A dollar? More than that. Two dollars? More than that — three dollars! All this he had collected by asking persons to put in their money to see how it would ring.

"Now, the only way you can get the chestnut out of this bottle is to hit it a crack." And a little girl out west who could n't speak quite plain heard the story, when she said : —

"'I should n't t'ink any body would want to hit such a pretty t'ing as dat a track. I dess I should n't.'"

At length all the bottles were disposed of and I ceased to repeat the story. But the end was not yet. A year or two afterward I received a letter from a gentleman in Pennsylvania, saying that he was connected with a county Sunday-school society, and that he had come across a little glass bottle with a chestnut in it. On learning its history, he thought it was a pity that its mission should cease, and so had it photographed ; and he sold them for twenty-five cents apiece, and he had raised one hundred dollars to buy books for his poor schools.

He sent me a photograph, and said perhaps I could use it in the same way. I had it copied, and in a year or two disposed of some thousands at twenty-five cents each. I did not sell them, but after telling the story and showing the picture, I offered to give it to any who might want it to remember the poor woman, who would make a donation of twenty-five cents to our Society.

Now the pecuniary result of all this is, that not far from two thousand dollars have come to the Sabbath-school cause from these one hundred and fifty chestnuts. Has not God blessed the mite of this poor woman?

But this is not all. Similar cases have grown out of it. The case connected with the Sanitary Commission during the war, in which a "sack of flour" was sold over and over till quite a sum was realized, no doubt grew out of this chestnut story.

Then this story became widely known. Years ago I received from some unknown person in Port Natal, South Africa, six square letter sheets of paper, in which were secured beautiful bouquets of dried grasses and flowers of that country. They were all inscribed to me, some in the language of the people there. On one of them was written : —

"May they do as much good as did the poor woman's chestnuts."

Just as though it had become my business to go round the country and sell whatever any one might send me for the cause of benevolence!

The chestnut story was a "providential story." The little girl who was with Mrs. Nurse when they came across the little pile of chestnuts jumped up and clapped her hands, saying, "Isn't God good to drop them down here for us?" So I called the nuts "providential chestnuts." I am not to blame for the wonderful results. All I at first sought was to get enough to show the poor woman that "God had blessed them."

Mr. Constantine made us a visit while this story was before the people. In the evening we cracked some of the walnuts picked by the little boy of his school. When he left he asked for a few to keep. I gave him a handful.

He visited Washington soon after, and one Sabbath day addressed a mission school in the city and told the story

of his own school at the corner, and of the chestnuts.
He exhibited a specimen of the walnuts, when two of the
teachers bought each of them one and gave him two dollars
apiece.   He gave me the four dollars for the Society.   I
told my family "not to crack another one of those walnuts for any thing, for they were very valuable!"   In a
short time, however, I gave them permission to crack
them, on the ground that I could n't run two wheelbar-
rows at once.   And so the whole matter has now come to
a close.

The story illustrates the importance of little things, of
little actions, right or wrong ones.   "Behold, how great a
matter a little fire kindleth!"

Perhaps I should add that in 1864 I wrote a volume for
the society of over one hundred and twenty pages, called
"The Sabbath-school Chestnuts."   It had an extensive sale,
but is now out of print.

CHAPTER XVII.

INCIDENTS IN HOME LIFE.

Our Home and Family.

DURING our first year in Boston we made our home with a private family in the city. Here our first-born died a few days after birth. The second year our home was in the family of the late Rev. Jared Curtis, chaplain of the State Prison, in Charlestown. I often officiated for him in his absence.

We united with the Winthrop Church in Charlestown, then under the pastoral care of the late Rev. Daniel Crosby. During a long illness of the pastor, Mr. Curtis and myself took charge of the prayer-meetings ; and at this time there was unusual religious interest among the people. The invalid pastor, in a very humble and submissive tone of voice, said : —

" How mysterious it is that the Lord should thus visit my people when I am shut off from my work ! "

But we were only entering into his work. He had been most faithfully sowing the good seed of the Word, and we were now permitted to help gather in some of the harvest.

This year the eldest of our children now living was born. We now felt that it was best to establish a home of our own. One day I said to Mrs. Bullard : —

" I have been to look at a house in the city I saw advertised to let.

" Well," she inquired, " what do you think of it ? "

" The house is a good-looking one and pleasantly

located, but I do not think we can afford to take it. The rent is two hundred dollars more than my salary! We should have to live very economically to get along, under those circumstances." So little we understood in regard to this part of the expense of housekeeping in the city!

We finally obtained a house in Barton Street, in the extreme western part of the city. Here we resided for five years; and here two of our other children were born. Then we kept house five years in Poplar Street, Boston. And here our youngest child was born.

In full view of our home was the fine building of the Massachusetts General Hospital. At first it was regarded as quite an attraction to our limited city prospect. But when we came to learn what a hospital meant, — that it is constantly the scene of suffering and pain; that here the surgeon's instruments are in almost daily use, — much of the attraction vanished. We looked upon the massive structure with a very different sensation.

One day a nurse in one of the wards of the hospital, who was a member of Bowdoin Street Church, then under the pastoral care of the late Rev. Hubbard Winslow, and to which church we had removed our church relations, sent for me to visit one of her patients, a young woman who was in an inquiring state of mind. I visited her and gave her such instruction as her case seemed to require and prayed with her. On leaving I was urged, both by the patient and her nurse, to call again. In a few days the visit was repeated. The same request, still more urgently, was made. After a few visits more, it appeared that the nurse and patient — and, indeed, several other patients in that and two or three other wards that I had visited — were anticipating the visits more and more, and were disappointed if many days passed without any. To obviate this state of things, the officials of the hospital kindly arranged for my visit each week, on a day when general visitors were not admitted.

After this, for a year or two, I visited five or six wards every week, when my official duties did not call me from the city. I went from ward to ward, spoke a few words to every patient, trying to cheer the desponding and guide and direct the minds of the inquiring as best I was able. Then I read a few verses of Scripture and offered a short prayer.

It was often very affecting to see how the countenances of the patients, the convalescent and also those most severely ill, even those who had but recently passed through the most painful operation, would brighten up as I entered the ward. Many of these patients were Catholics, but all seemed interested to hear the few sweet words of the blessed Book and the voice of prayer.

It was thought that several of the patients, in connection with these services, were led to trust in the Great Physician, and that not a few who had learned to put their trust in him were cheered and comforted.

This hour or more, in which so many short services were crowded, was very fatiguing, but the interest manifested made it an occasion of great personal enjoyment and spiritual good to myself.

As my early years were passed in the country and on the farm, and as I had learned to love every green thing and every living creature, the confinement amid the brick walls, narrow streets, and limited views of the city became more and more oppressive, and we finally decided to seek a residence in some rural place in the vicinity.

My first visit of inspection was in Cambridge. After

some inquiries in different parts of the town, — it was not then a city, — I came to a man on Dana Hill, just opposite Centre Street. He was fixing a gate. To the inquiry if there was any house in the neighborhood either to let or to sell, he replied that he did not know of any. After a few moments of general conversation he said : —

"There is a man down there in Centre Street getting into his wagon, who does let and sell houses."

I had just time to hail him. And that house out of which he had come has been our "Sunnybank" home for forty years! What important events were suspended on that brief moment of time! An instant more and that man would have been beyond my call. Then where would have been our home? How different, in many respects, might have been my life and that of my family! Here, at Harvard University, a son obtained his collegiate and much of his medical education ; and here three daughters obtained their education in a high school that is equal to almost any, if not indeed to any, academy in the land. Here, too, in a location with all that is desirable in rural life, we are within easy access to the city and the place of my official labors.

Our Present Home and How We Paid for It.

OUR dwelling is on a lot of about one third of an acre. As it stands on an elevated terrace, where the sun always shines, when it shines at all, and as we try to have it always shine inside, we call it "Sunnybank."

When we took possession of this new home, we found every tree and vine and shrub on the place had been neglected, and weeds had general possession. For the mere pleasure of work and of seeing the improvement that would follow it, as well as for the needed exercise, for

many years, through all the seasons for such labor, I
spent from two to three hours before breakfast nearly
every morning in earnest labor on these neglected
grounds. They soon showed the effect of this labor.
An Irish gardener, in passing, often looked with great
interest on this early labor, and noticed the magical
changes that were constantly going on. One morning,
a little after four o'clock, he stopped and watched the
quick and energetic motions of this gentleman laborer for
a moment, and then exclaimed : —

"Ye're the only gintleman in Cambridge ! "

I said in reply that if all the gentlemen in town did
their own gardening in that way, he would probably
sing another song.

At the end of two years the place was so improved that,
with the advice of friends, it was purchased. Only
about one quarter of the cost was paid down ; the rest was
encumbered by the ornament which the little girl said her
father was going to put on his house next week — a
mortgage !

Now there was a new motive for economy in the household, and for the adoption of every suitable measure, not
only to pay the interest, but also to lessen the principal.
The interest was only about one quarter what the rent
would have been most of the next twenty years ; and by
the small sums, from time to time endorsed on the note,
this was yearly growing less and less.

At the end of about twenty years the mortgage was
canceled and the homestead was free ! No one who has
not experienced it can conceive the joy and gladness with
which the whole household hailed that important event.

On reckoning up the original cost and interest, including also some two thousand dollars for additional and

various improvements to the house and the grounds, and also the expense for necessary repairs, shingling, painting, etc., it was found that they amounted to just about the same the rent for those years would have done ; but had I been paying rent, I should have had no homestead.

That is the way I obtained our homestead, which is now worth much more than it was when purchased. Besides, the amount of comfort the family have had in the thought that it was our own, or would be erelong, has been worth more than all the economy, careful contrivance, and even sacrifice, it has cost to secure it.

In a place where real estate promises to increase rather than diminish in value I would advise all professional men with any fair prospect of permanency in their location to purchase a home at the outset. If the whole must be mortgaged, the interest will not equal the rent.

Concentrated Labor.

From my experience on my little plat of land I have been led to think much upon the importance of concentrated labor. It seems to me that most farmers in New England have too much land. Their labor and their fertilizers are extended over too many acres.

At the west, where fertilizers are not needed, where taxes upon lands are small, and where agriculture is engaged in on a large scale and almost every part of it done by machinery, it is different. There one farmer may have his thousands of acres of corn and wheat and make a profitable business of it. But with us here in New England, if the labor, manure, fencing, etc., that are now expended on many a farm were concentrated from one third to one half, or even more, the results, it is believed, would be greater than now. At the same time much expense for fencing and taxes would be saved, and the better cultivation of the land would make all the labor easier and in every way more satisfactory.

It is truly wonderful how much labor may be usefully expended on a small piece of land, and what large results will follow. The following illustration of the effects of concentrated labor of this kind may be interesting to some New England farmers, and especially to some small land-owners.

The farm on which this labor has been performed contains about one third of an acre. The house and barn, the walks, grass-plats, borders and beds for shrubbery and flowers, take about one half of the lot. On the remaining seven thousand feet there are three cherry-trees, four apple-trees, seven peach-trees, forty pear-trees (of some thirty different kinds, some of the trees having two or more kinds), one hundred grape-vines of eighteen different varieties (many of these vines are on trellises around the house and barn), one hundred hills of currants between the trees and between the rows of trees (yielding last year three bushels of currants), fifty hills of raspberries between the rows of trees, and a few dozen hills of tomatoes.

Almost all these trees, vines, and bushes are in bearing condition and yield abundantly. From this little spot there has been gathered this season at least sixty bushels of fruit.

The cost for enriching this small spot of land has been but little beyond the cost of the few loads of loam each autumn for the compost heap, as most of the dressing has been made on the place of coal ashes. And there has been but little expense for hired labor except for a few days in the spring and autumn for spading the ground and getting out the dressing.

This is a specimen of the results of concentrated labor. It is doubtful if the same amount of labor and fertilizers expended over several acres of the same kind of land would have given as good results.

An Hour in a Garden.

SOME of my most pleasant and perhaps profitable meditations have occurred while working in my little garden. I seldom prune my vines without thinking of that beautiful saying of our Saviour: "I am the vine, and ye are the branches."

A single hour of labor and care in a garden — how wondrous its results! With pruning-knife and shears and matting, how soon an ill-shaped, unsightly tree or shrub is changed into an object of symmetry and grace! An hour among the vines, properly arranging them on the trellis, and checking their too luxuriant growth so that their vital forces may be employed in developing the luscious clusters — how marked its influence! A brief season of care among the flowers and plants, giving to the weak and drooping the needed support, removing the hurtful insects and weeds, loosing the hardened soil about the roots, and by judicious pinching and pruning bringing them to forms of comeliness and beauty — how it pays, and how satisfactory as we look at the effects! And then, as with hoe and rake we pass through the paths and walks, and among the trees and shrubs and plants, what a transformation it produces! And how smooth and velvety the lawn over which has passed the mower! Such are the effects of an hour, now and then, of thoughtful care and labor in the garden and grounds that grace and beautify and cheer our dwellings. The more frequent these seasons, the less labor and care it will require to keep all in perfect order, while only a few omissions will show to every passer-by the evidences of neglect.

How sad that any — when it costs so little time and labor — should, through sloth, want of taste, thought-lessness, or indifference, leave their surroundings to become unsightly, overgrown with noxious weeds, and a confused mass of tangled vines and shrubbery.

And an hour of labor and care in the garden of the heart is not less wondrous in its effects than in the natural garden. How a season spent in earnest communion with the Scriptures or some devotional book, in meditation, self-examination, and prayer, helps to give vigor and beauty to all the Christian graces! How it checks the growth of worldliness, and pride, and love of ease, and selfishness, and directs the forces of the soul to the growth and development and sweetness of all the fruits of the Spirit — love, joy, peace, long-suffering, gentleness, goodness, faith, meekness, temperance! How such a season helps to remove doubts and fears, and to strengthen and support a weak and trembling hope and a wavering faith!

Without such seasons of labor and care, how soon all the avenues of the spiritual garden become unsightly, and every hurtful weed springs up to choke the delicate plants of righteousness, and the whole scene becomes a waste — no beautiful flowers or luscious fruits or pleasant objects appear.

Frequent seasons of watchfulness and care are more needful here than in our natural gardens. Every good plant in the heart is an exotic, requiring much watch-fulness and protection, while the hurtful ones that we have to destroy are in their native soil. They spring up spontaneously, and grow up without culture. The scorching sun, the withering drought, the desolating hail, the sweeping tempest, the noxious insect, seldom injures them. They are as tenacious of life as are the vexatious purslane and witch-grass that again and again we root up from our flower-beds. Nothing but the most persistent efforts can check and eradicate them.

And yet we can have more certainty of success in the culture of the heart than in that of the most favored garden spot on earth. Every hour we spend there we can have divine help. The great Gardener will give us his aid. He will send the dew and the sunshine and the gentle rain, if we faithfully watch over and care for the plants, that will insure their growth and fruitfulness.

Let us only be as regular and earnest in the care of our hearts as most lovers of nature are of their gardens, and the north wind will awake, and the south wind will come and blow upon them, that the spices thereof may flow out, and He whom our souls love will come into his garden and eat his pleasant fruit.

Silver Wedding.

THE twenty-fifth anniversary of our wedding occurred May 16, 1857. This anniversary we had known was called in some countries in Europe the " silver wedding." We had never heard of the celebration of this anniversary under that name in New England.

It seemed to us proper that the event should be recognized, and so we issued cards of invitation to a large number of our friends and acquaintances to call on us at our "Sunnybank" home in Cambridge on that occasion. On the corner of the card of invitation were the words "SILVER WEDDING," to indicate the event the gathering was to celebrate.

Many of the papers, secular and religious, gave very pleasant accounts of the occasion. It will interest at least our special friends — and it may not be improper — to give some specimens of these notices.

The Boston Journal spoke thus of it : —

We know of no person who can rejoice in the possession of the deep and heartfelt affection of a larger number of friends, of all ages— from the little child barely able to lisp the Lord's Prayer, to the aged saints ready to enter upon the bliss of heaven — and scattered all over New England, than the Rev. Asa Bullard, the devoted and beloved Secretary of the Massachusetts Sabbath-School Society. There are very few persons who have been connected with any Congregational Sabbath-school in Massachuetts during the last twenty years, who can not recall the kind words of counsel and instruction to which they have listened with eager interest as they fell from his lips, and the good resolutions which they have aided in forming or strengthening. This great multitude of friends will be pleased to know that last Saturday was the twenty-fifth anniversary of the marriage of Mr. Bullard, and at this event, the silver wedding, as it is termed, was commemorated by a social gathering of his friends in this vicinity at his residence in Cambridge last evening. Notwithstanding the un- pleasant weather, there was a general response to the invitations sent out, the visitors filling the house to overflowing, and a more happy assemblage we have never seen.

The evening was spent in social conversation and congratulations. About nine o 'clock a bounteous collation was provided. At a season- able hour the company retired, with the sincere and heartfelt wish that their beloved friend and host, and his excellent and worthy companion, with their children, may all be spared to celebrate a golden wedding.

A number of the Cambridge friends of Mr. and Mrs. Bullard, desirous that the celebration of the silver wedding should be something more than a mere social gathering for an hour, placed upon their parlor table a rich and beautiful silver tea-set appropriately inscribed. Other friends contributed other gifts. Three "little friends" of Mr. Bullard added a fine copy of Gray's Poems. These testimonials of affection were as gratifying as they were unexpected to the recipients.

As many parents who were present expressed a wish that their children might have enjoyed the occasion, on Independence Day, July 4, we invited the members of the Sabbath-schools of the Shepard Church, of which the late Rev. J. A. Albro, D.D., was pastor, and of the Prospect Street Church, of which Rev. C. W. Gilman was then pastor, to spend the afternoon at our home.

The Boston Journal gave the following account of that gathering : —

One of the most pleasant gatherings of the day took place in Cambridge Saturday afternoon, at the residence of Rev. Asa Bullard, the Secretary of the Massachusetts Sabbath-School Society. It was a kind of sequel to the silver wedding of this most estimable man, an account of which we gave a few weeks ago. At that gathering, which was composed entirely of adults, the question was asked why the children were not present. The best answer was that there was not room for them then. Their kind friend, Mr. Bullard, had not, however, forgotten them, and was looking forward to Independence Day, when he hoped to meet them in the beautiful grounds attached to his residence. Accordingly an invitation was last Sunday extended to the scholars connected with the two Congregtional Sabbath-schools in Cambridge, to meet their friend and the "children's friend" at his house, on Saturday afternoon. The invitation was heartily responded to, and about four o 'clock bright-eyed happy-faced little ones began to assemble, and kept coming until there were four or five hundred of them present. Several of the boys and girls brought beautiful bouquets of flowers and handed them to Mr. Bullard as he greeted them on their entrance. A delegation of girls from Rev. Dr. Albro's school were dressed in white, and had their heads wreathed in flowers. As they entered they handed Mr. Bullard two neat cases, which were found to contain a splendid silver pie-knife and other articles of silver ware, which were inscribed: "Shepard Sabbath-school, Cambridge, to Rev. Asa Bullard." Mr. Bullard acknowledged the kind gift in a few appropriate words.

After the company were all assembled they were allowed an hour to play about the grounds and have a good time. An ample collation was then served out to them, and after they were satisfied, brief addresses were made to them by Rev. Mr. Gilman, Rev. Mr. Bullard, Deacon Hosmer, superintendent of the Shepard school, Hon. Charles Theodore Russell, and Rev. Dr. Albro. Before separating, the children gave three hearty cheers as an acknowledgment of their appreciation of the generous hospitality of their kind-hearted friend. The occasion was a delightful one to all who were present.

The Cambridge Chronicle, after giving an account of the above gathering, added the following : —

The sequel to the whole occurred on Monday evening last, when quite unexpectedly to the recipient, Mr. Bullard was visited by the superintendent and teachers of Rev. Mr. Gilman's Sabbath-school, and received from the superintendent a silken purse containing twenty-five dollars in gold. The purse was of blue, pink, and white, emblematic of " friendship, love, and purity," and was bestowed as a token of the love and esteem of the members of the school. The superintendent of the infant department, in behalf of her little flock, also presented Mr. Bullard with a beautiful fancy parlor chair, as a token of their regard.

"The matter of gifts," *The Chronicle* says, "is by no means a necessary part of a celebration like the above. If a couple have been spared by a kind providence to walk together in the wedded life twenty-five years, and have honored that sacred and endeared relation by a faithful observance of all the holy vows of the marriage covenant, as sharers of each other's joys, and sympathizers and supporters in each other's sorrows, what more appropriate than to invite their friends, or for their friends if they prefer, to go uninvited, to celebrate by mutual congratulations such an interesting event? We sincerely pity all our bachelor friends who are willfully denying themselves all prospect of such joyous occasions."

Another Silver Wedding.

IN *The Well-Spring* for February 25, 1859, was published the following article : —

It is not common for such an anniversary — a silver wedding — to occur twice in the life of the same person; and certainly not twice within two years. But if spared till Monday, March 1, 1859, we shall have been married just twenty-five years to the Massachusetts Sabbath-School Society. That will be our second silver wedding.

Now, if it were a pleasant season of the year, and we could procure a tent large enough, it would give us the greatest pleasure to have another silver wedding levee, and invite all of the two hundred thousand different boys and girls, young people and men and women, whom we have publicly addressed — and most of them many times — during the past quarter of a century, to come and exchange greetings with the " man who makes *The Well-Spring.*"

But as this can not well be done, will all this great number of friends who " remain unto this present" (alas! what a multitude of them are fallen asleep!) accept our most heartfelt greetings and good wishes? Many thanks for all the kind interest they have manifested in us and in our labors. . . .

Though our labors for the past quarter of a century have been abundant, they have been very delightful. Few men have had a more delightful work than ours. Think, young friends, of the pleasure we have enjoyed in preparing this little paper, through which, every week, we have been speaking to more than 150,000 readers — parents, teachers, and children. You can not be more happy in your most exciting amusements than we have been in this work.

And then all our other duties, of correspondence, making reports, preparing books for the Society, etc., during the week, have also been, as a general thing, pleasant. And then think, too, of our opportunities the past twenty-five years, in connection with this Society, and for three years previous, in connection with the Maine Sabbath-school Union, on the Sabbath and at conferences and Sabbath-school conventions and festivals, of meeting and addressing these many, many thousands of parents and children! What work can be more delightful?

Golden Wedding.

Our golden wedding, or the fiftieth anniversary of our marriage, came May 16, 1882. As our friends had done so much for me in connection with my visit abroad, and fearing that a special celebration of our jubilee might lead to further gifts, it was quietly observed among a few of our relatives.

Rev. Daniel D. Tappan wrote to me on the occasion of our golden wedding as follows : —

WELD, Maine, April 27, 1882.

MY BROTHER BULLARD: —

I see in *The Congregationalist* a fraternal suggestion in relation to the "Golden Mile-stone" on the 16th of May; and on the score of long acquaintance send the enclosed lines. We have, as you well know, been more or less acquainted a long time; indeed, perhaps as long as you have personally known any of the friends who will greet you on that interesting anniversary. I was present, as you may remember, at your ordination in Portland in 1832, and took some small part, I think, in the service. . . .

I presume you are both in fair health; and I opine you will not hasten to feel old, and that the same will not soon occur, unless the "tabernacle" receive some great wrench.

Very best wishes for yourself and Mrs. Bullard.

Your brother,

DANIEL D. TAPPAN,

Aged eighty-three years and a half.

Thou veteran children's friend, thy years
  'Mid tireless cares have sped away;
And times of blended joys and tears
  Have ushered in this restful day.

And this associate at thy side,
  In worthy deeds and love has shone,
Since when, now fifty years, as bride,
  She linked her fortunes with thine own.

The glory His, and grateful love
  May well remind of sovereign grace,
That helped you train, for seats above,
  Such numbers of the rising race.

And now, not in inglorious ease
  You cease from former robust care;
Yet, young in heart, still aim to please
  The Master, and for heaven prepare.

But be your exit soon or late,
  Its closing scene may Christ illume;
Fit harbinger of bliss so great,
  Reserved for saints beyond the tomb.

D. D. TAPPAN.

The Great Sorrow of my Life.

ABOUT three years after the above interesting anniversary, my beloved wife was stricken with paralysis. After four or five months of almost perfect helplessness, during which she was most patient and never more loving and lovable, and when we felt that she was slowly but surely improving and was to be restored to us in health, on Sabbath morning, July 19, 1885, without the least warning, she was suddenly taken from us, as if in a moment translated — "a noble woman glorified." We had walked together in this most endearing of all earthly relations fifty-three years and two months.

Among the many things for which we had occasion for thankfulness during these months of hope and fear, was the visit of our son, William R. Bullard, M.D., from Helena, Montana. He came sixteen hundred miles, and for two weeks our family was again reunited. We had not seen him for sixteen years. He has a wife and a pair of children thirteen years old, whom we have never seen except in their picture.

Religion has never seemed more precious, as connected with the family, than as I contemplate it from my now stricken home. I thus moralize upon it : —

Sin has spread a withering blight over all the relations of life. Nowhere has its influence been more destructive than in the various relations of the family. And still, the united, affectionate family — even where the rains and dews of divine grace have never fallen — is one of the most verdant spots in our world. Here one common bond of sympathy and love binds all hearts together. The dear names of father and mother, sister and brother, are music to each other's ears. Each helps bear the other's burdens. Envy and selfishness seem to have so far yielded to the power of even natural, unsanctified affection, that the happiness of each is to see the others happy. This is, indeed, a comparatively green spot in the midst of a surrounding desert.

But let the rains of heaven be shed down upon this spot, and what a change! A more abundant luxuriance now springs forth on every side, and it is clothed with a far deeper verdure and a far richer beauty. Religion purifies and sweetens all the tender and endearing relations of such a family. It adds a silken cord to the bonds of sympathy and love. It diffuses a softening, hallowed influence among all its members, and makes the good parent, the obedient child, the affectionate brother and sister, the amiable companion, a better parent, a more obedient, loving child, a more affectionate brother or sister, and a more amiable companion. Religion produces such a union of feeling and sentiment that a discordant note seldom mars the harmony of their lives. If one suffer, all suffer alike with him, and if one rejoice, all are made happy.

Religion erects, too, in the pious household, an altar around which all the members daily assemble with united and joyful hearts. The priest of the household now opens the Sacred Volume. The world for a little season is dismissed; every passion is hushed, every bosom quieted, every mind awake, and every thought is fixed. The words of eternal life fall upon the ear as if from the lips of the Almighty. The song of praise now unites every voice in sweet melody; then all bow in solemn prayer, and offer incense and a pure offering to their Maker. Here, around this altar, their union and love are most perfect and endearing.

> " Their souls, by love together knit,
>   Cemented, mixed in one,
>   One hope, one heart, one mind, one voice,
>   'T is heaven on earth begun."

If there is here below an emblem of the household of the blest, it surely is the united, affectionate, Christian family. What power there is in that religion that can make such a scene in such a sin-blighted world as this!

And there is efficacy in this religion, could it pervade every heart, to convert every family into such a scene ; to sweeten all the relations of kindred and friendship, and to change earth into heaven. God speed the day when all our homes shall be Christian homes.

Cambridge Reserve Guard.

EARLY in the late civil war in our country some of the leading citizens in Cambridge were led to organize a military company for the protection of our public institutions, buildings, etc. The company consisted mostly of men who on account of their age were not liable to be called into the service. The late George Livermore, Esq., one of the most highly respected men in the city, met me one day, mentioned the subject of this company and its special object, and inquired if I would be willing to unite with it. I at once replied " Certainly."

The thought that there might by-and-by be a draft, and that some might be inclined to resist and excite mobs, and the exposure of our arsenal and all our public buildings, as well as our private dwellings and personal safety, seemed a good reason for every loyal citizen to be ready to organize for protection.

At first about one hundred united with the company; but when we came to organize regularly and to obtain the uniform and other equipments, the number was reduced to about sixty.

After meeting a few weeks under a drill-master, the company organized by choice of officers. Very much to my surprise I was chosen first lieutenant. I at once obtained Casey's volumes of infantry tactics, and in my spare moments gave myself to an earnest study. In a short time I was elected captain, and for twenty-two months did not fail to meet my company every Monday evening and drill them for an hour or more.

This company was composed of clergymen, lawyers, physicians, merchants, teachers, presidents and cashiers of banks, and of the leading citizens of our part of the city. We aided in recruiting one or two companies and in awakening a general spirit of loyalty to our government and active sympathy with the north.

There were several events of interest that may be mentioned. The most important is that connected with the Cooper Street riot in Boston. Governor Andrew, Adjutant-general Schouler, and Mayor Richardson of our city one time called upon our company just at night to escort several loads of ammunition from the Cambridge arsenal into Boston, for a regiment just home from the war that was called upon to aid in protecting the city. Our company was under arms fifteen hours and marched ten miles, and we received the hearty thanks of the officials who called for our service.

We had a public parade and supper at the end of one year, which was an occasion of great interest.

The company at another time had a drill in the City Hall, at which there was a large gathering of citizens, including our lady friends. At this gathering Mayor Raymond, in behalf of the ladies of Cambridgeport, presented to the company a superb silk flag. This was properly acknowledged by an address from the captain, and afterwards suitable resolutions of acknowledgment were passed by the company and sent to the ladies.

At the close of the war the company disbanded. Some months afterwards the mayor of the city requested us to re-organize and aid in receiving two Cambridge companies which we had helped to recruit. Permission was obtained from the adjutant-general, and the company met a few times to prepare themselves for the service; and never was there a company of boys that seemed more happy to meet than were the members of the Cambridge Reserve Guard.

Four or five years after this, so many of the company had expressed a wish that there could be a reunion, I invited the members to an entertainment at my residence. About forty were present; and after they had participated in the refreshments provided, they greatly surprised their commander by presenting him, in connection with a neat and felicitous address by the president of the civil organization of the company, with an elegant Waltham watch appropriately inscribed.

Thus ended all public gatherings of our company. Some of our most intelligent and worthy citizens have said that there has been no organization in our city, outside of the church, that did more to promote kind and neighborly feelings among its members than the Cambridge Reserve Guard. No persons in the city meet me more cordially than the members of this company. Some of them, even

after these years, always address me as "captain," with
the military salute.

Cambridge Horticultural Society.

FOR several years we had a large and efficient horticultural society. There were many very excellent pear-
orchards, especially in Cambridgeport. A large portion
of the prizes given by the Massachusetts Horticultural
Society were obtained by the citizens of Cambridge.

This society, some portions of the year, held monthly
exhibitions, which were largely attended. The displays
of fruits and flowers and vegetables were extensive and
very fine. Many small prizes were given. One year a
citizen offered prizes to the ladies of the city for the best
specimens of bread. One hundred and sixty competitors
exhibited two hundred loaves. The committee of two
gentlemen and three ladies spent five hours in their examination. A loaf, to receive a prize, must be of good color,
well shaped, of fine appearance, without external defect,
sweet to the smell and taste, well raised, delicate, tender,
and handsome. Outwardly and inwardly each loaf must
not only satisfy but please sight, touch, smell, and taste,
every sense but hearing, and must be of a specified weight.
It was to me a matter of no small satisfaction that the
second prize for "fine flour wheaten bread" was awarded
to Mrs. Bullard.

After some years many of the fruit orchards had given
place to house-lots, and as most of the members were
connected with the Massachusetts Horticultural Society,
it was deemed best to disband the Cambridge society;
and this was done, to my no small regret, when I was its
last president. On closing up the institution, a large
number of the volumes in the library were given to the

Massachusetts Horticultural Society, and the rest were purchased by the individual members of the Cambridge society. We also made a donation of about $500 of the balance on hand to the Avon Street Home in our city. Thus closed an organization which had been quite popular in the city and which had been the means of awakening no small interest in beautifying the grounds of many a home.

Social Relations in Cambridge.

My social relations to the people in Cambridge, of all religious denominations, have ever been pleasant. I have preached in all the evangelical pulpits and addressed the Sabbath-schools. Our military organization, spoken of elsewhere, helped not a little in promoting social intercourse.

For fifteen or twenty years we have had a book club of twenty-one families, of which, most of the time, I have been the librarian. For some years we had monthly meetings at each other's houses, with a simple entertainment. This, of course, brought all the members of these families together in the most pleasant social intercourse.

I have often been brought into a more tender connection with not a few families in their bereavements. In the time of the ministerial vacations, I am often called upon in the absence of the pastors to conduct funeral services. One vacation, in twelve days I was called upon seven times to perform such services.

The First Baptist Church, Cambridgeport, lost two houses of worship by fire within a few years of each other. At the laying of the corner-stone and at the dedication of each, the society very courteously invited me to be present.

Church Relations in Cambridge.

WHEN we took up our residence in Cambridge, about forty years ago, Mrs. Bullard and myself moved our church relations to the Shepard Church, then under the pastoral care of the late Rev. J. A. Albro, D.D. For many years Dr. Albro was an active member of the Board of Managers of our Sabbath-School Society, and one of my tried friends and counselors in my work.

For several years Mrs. Bullard was an invalid and unable to attend church, and I was seldom at home on the Sabbath. Our children were then quite young, and were obliged to go to church and Sunday-school alone.

It was not long before it was found that the connections of most of our neighbors were with Cambridgeport rather than with Old Cambridge. All the school children were also in that ward; with them were all the associates of our own children. They soon found this out, and that they were every Sabbath day sent away from all their associates on the week-days and in the public schools. This they soon took very sorely to heart. They said: "The church and the Sabbath-school were especially for them, and not for their parents, who seldom were with them." This plea we could not long resist. Their application to go to the Prospect Street Church and Sabbath-school — then under the pastoral care of the late Rev. William A. Stearns, D.D., soon after president of Amherst College — seemed to us reasonable, and so we removed our church relations to the Prospect Street, or the "First Evangelical Church of Cambridgeport," in November, 1857, where we have since had our church home.

A few years ago our church voted to have six instead of four deacons, to hold office three years. They could be reëlected once, but must then be out of office one year before they were again eligible. At the first election two were chosen for three years, two for two years, and two for one year. I was first elected to this office for one year, and then reëlected for three. As for a few years at that time I was relieved from my labors on the Sabbath for the Sabbath-School Society, I could perform the duties of the diaconate. Although some thought it hardly appropriate for one of the clerical profession to accept the office of a deacon, it seemed to me proper to accept any position in the church where I could be useful; and while in that office there was the most fraternal sympathy and coöperation among these officers of the church. Our prayer-meeting every Saturday evening before the communion was to us all a hallowed season.

I have tried to take my place in all our church work, much of the time serving on some of the committees.

DIED

APRIL 5, 1888,

Rev. Asa Bullard,

AT "SUNNYBANK," CAMBRIDGEPORT, MASS.

ÆT. 84 YEARS, 10 DAYS.

IN MEMORIAM.

BY M. C. HAZARD.

WE speak and write of ourselves in the present tense, and soon others speak and write of us in the past; we tell now what we have done and what we are doing, and in a short time others will tell only of what we have done; autobiographies quickly give place to epitaphs.

Thoughts like these will occur to those who, in reading this volume, turn from the pages in which the author personally addresses them, to these in which another speaks for him. In the preceding pages he is the animated, vivacious friend, telling his life-story to a circle of friends; in these his voice is hushed, and he himself here lives only in hearts and memories. The change as it appears in this volume is not more sudden and startling than was the fact it represents. Mr. Bullard passed away soon after completing his autobiography. After submitting it to the writer he never saw it again. On the Monday appointed for a conference concerning all the items pertaining to its publication, Mr. Bullard failed to appear, and the writer heard that he was prostrated with pneumonia, the result of a severe cold taken in the prosecution of the work to which he had given his whole heart and life. A few days more and he had entered into rest.

Concerning his sickness and death there is but little to say. There was little that was striking or dramatic about the manner of his passing away. After coming under the power of the disease which overmastered him, he was delirious to the end, and hence there were no touching conferences with children and friends, such as would have been pleasant to relate and a comfort to them to have in memory. Before his illness Mr. Bullard had said his last words. His autobiography may be said to contain them. That now has somewhat of that sacred character which we attach to parting words.

Monday, March 19, Mr. Bullard returned home from one of his appointments with a cold which soon settled upon his chest, and which caused him to suffer somewhat from rheumatism. The rheumatic pains soon passed away, but the soreness in his chest continued. Mr. Bullard was not a man to give up readily to sickness. He was engaged to present the cause of the Society on the next Sunday in New Haven at Dr. Twitchell's church. Having disappointed Dr. Twitchell once before, his heart was the more set upon fulfilling his engagement then. As the end of the week drew near it was evident to every one in the family but himself that he could not go. Friday his daughters urged him to write at once reporting his condition, but he refused. On Saturday morning his son-in-law, Mr. C. F. Wyman, found him sitting up in bed eating his breakfast, bright and cheerful, but clearly too weak for any such exertion as he contemplated. Asking if he could do any thing for him, Mr. Wyman received for a reply: " Nothing, unless you can contrive to give me a better appetite !" When Mr. Wyman remarked, " Of course you have given up all hope of going to New Haven to-day," very emphatically Mr. Bullard answered: " Of course *not !* I feel that I must go. I have thought over it, and prayed over it, and it seems clear to me that I must go. Besides, I can not bear to disappoint Dr. Twitchell a second time."

Further remonstrances proved unavailing. It was suggested to him that he was like a boy who insisted upon skating upon ice only an inch thick, and, with the old-time twinkle in his eye, he replied : "Oh, ice an inch thick will bear quite a weight!" His son-in-law bade him good-by, saying that if he made the attempt to go, he should expect never again to see him alive. The warning was received with a hearty laugh and a cheerful "Good-by !"

On rising to dress, however, Mr. Bullard found himself weaker than he had supposed. He did dress, though, in spite of his weakness, and even went so far as to shave himself. But then it was apparent even to himself that he could not go. Giving permission to send a telegram announcing his inability to fulfill his appointment, he turned to the window, and — do you wonder at it ? — tears coursed down his cheeks. It was hard for him to surrender his work, perhaps forever. "Now," said he, turning sadly to his daughter, "I am afraid that I shall give up to it."

It was impossible for him not to give up to it. The disease very soon developed into typhoid pneumonia. Delirium almost immediately set in. The incoherent words which dropped from his lips showed that all the while he was engaged in his work. His lips moved without cessation, and from the broken fragments of speech it was easily gathered that he was imagining himself preaching a sermon, or speaking to children, or offering prayer. It touched the hearts of his daughters to hear once from him the petition : "If it be Thy pleasure, continue us in our labors." His work — how precious it was to him ! Again, they heard a portion of the prayer which is the first to be learned and the last to be forgotten : —

> " Now I lay me down to sleep,
>   I pray the Lord my soul to keep."

No devout soul will ever grow too old to say that. The last intelligible words were heard from him on the day of his departure. In the forenoon he was observed to fold his hands in prayer, and distinctly was given the supplication: "God bless us all!" And with that the feeble hands fell, and soon this father in Israel fell on sleep. It was as if in entering the unseen chariot which waited for him he had in that last prayer left a benediction behind him.

The funeral took place on Monday, April 9, at the First Church of Cambridgeport, Rev. D. N. Beach pastor. As noted in his autobiography, here for over thirty years he had had his church home. The services were peculiarly fitting both in character and in spirit. All those things which make such occasions sorrowful and depressing in this case were lacking. There was, on the contrary, a solemn and joyous uplift which was very noticeable. The simple ceremonies at the house were pervaded with the spirit of thanksgiving and praise instead of grief and anguish. At the church this frame of mind was even more marked. The bell was not tolled, for a sound so doleful did not seem appropriate under the circumstances. Ringing rather than tolling would have been more in consonance with the feelings of those who gathered there to do him honor. The flowers which filled the platform even to the hiding of the pulpit expressed the feelings of all better than the black drapings. The profusion of floral offerings was an indication of the affection in which Mr. Bullard has been held, and of the many hearts which had been touched by the news of his death. From his associates in the Congregational Sunday-School and Publishing Society there was a floral book, all the leaves of which, significantly, were turned, and on the final leaf, the words: "In Labors Abundant." Very truly did those words characterize the long life just closed. A superb cross of Easter lilies from the Congregational Superintendents' Union was a reminder of the Easter message to the Saviour's sorrowing disciples: "He is not here; for he is risen." Another open book from the Sunday-school of the church had upon its pages the appropriate words: "The Lord is my Shepherd," and "Feed my Lambs." From the church with which he was connected was a cross and crown, suggesting the cross now forever laid down and the crown in joyful possession. Besides these there were many bouquets and smaller designs; but, after all, no offerings were quite so touching as the tiny bunches of flowers dropped into the coffin from the hands of little children as they passed by. Children had ever been his care, and he had ever been held by them in warmest esteem. There should have been more children present. Had the invitation been widely given, as would have been appropriate, they would have filed by the coffin in a long procession, eager to take a last look at their white-haired friend. They should have been there.

The church was well filled by those who had known and loved Mr. Bullard as a neighbor, associate, and Christian worker. The Board of Directors of the Society with which he had been so long connected was present; the Congregational Superintendents' Union was represented by many of its members; the officials of many of the benevolent societies were among the audience; Boston and Cambridge and the adjoining suburban towns sent goodly delegations of clergymen and prominent lay workers.

Of course the church and neighborhood did not miss the opportunity to show their love and respect for their neighbor and friend.

The services varied from the usual form observed on funeral occasions. Quite happily it was planned that, instead of the customary sermon, there should be several informal addresses, which should draw their inspiration from Mr. Bullard's life, and which should be delivered by those who, in a manner, could represent the Society which he had served; the Superintendents' Union, of which he had been chaplain; the pastors of Boston and vicinity, among whom he had been a well-beloved brother, and the neighborhood in which he had so long dwelt. In accordance with this thought, Rev. A. E. Dunning, D.D., was asked, as its Secretary, to speak for the Congregational Sunday-School and Publishing Society; Mr. Charles W. Hill for the Congregational Superintendents' Union; Rev. A. H. Plumb, D.D., for the pastors of Boston and vicinity; Rev. Alexander McKenzie, D.D., for the friends and neighbors.

The following selections of Scripture were read by Rev. George A. Tewksbury, of the Pilgrim Church of Cambridgeport : —

I.

So Abijah slept with his fathers, and they buried him in the city of David : and Asa his son reigned in his stead. . . .

And Asa did that which was good and right in the eyes of the Lord his God :

For he . . . commanded Judah to seek the Lord God of their fathers, and to do the law and the commandment. — 2 Chron. 14: 1–4.

Hear, O Israel : the Lord our God is one Lord :

And thou shalt love the Lord thy God with all thine heart, and with all thy soul, and with all thy might.

And these words, which I command thee this day, shall be in thine heart:

And thou shalt teach them diligently unto thy children, and shalt talk of them when thou sittest in thine house, and when thou walkest by the way, and when thou liest down, and when thou risest up.

And thou shalt bind them for a sign upon thine hand, and they shall be as frontlets between thine eyes.

And thou shalt write them upon the posts of thy house, and on thy gates. — Deut. 6: 4-9.

Gather the people together, men, and women, and children, and thy stranger that is within thy gates, that they may hear, and that they may learn, and fear the Lord your God, and observe to do all the words of this law. — Deut. 31: 12.

Train up a child in the way he should go: and when he is old, he will not depart from it. — Prov. 22: 6.

Children, obey your parents in the Lord: for this is right.

Honour thy father and mother; which is the first commandment with promise;

That it may be well with thee, and thou mayest live long on the earth.

And, ye fathers, provoke not your children to wrath: but bring them up in the nurture and admonition of the Lord. — Eph. 6: 1-4.

II.

And Asa . . . built fenced cities in Judah: for the land had rest, and he had no war in those years; because the Lord had given him rest.

Therefore he said unto Judah, Let us build these cities, and make about them walls, and towers, gates and bars, while the land is yet before us; because we have sought the Lord our God, we have sought him, and he hath given us rest on every side. So they built and prospered.

And Asa had an army of men that bare targets and spears, out of Judah three hundred thousand; and out of Benjamin, that bare shields and drew bows, two hundred and fourscore thousand: all of these were mighty men of valour.

And there came out against them Zerah the Ethiopian with an host of a thousand thousand, and three hundred chariots. . . .

And Asa cried unto the Lord his God, and said, Lord, it is nothing with thee to help, whether with many, or with them that have no power: help us, O Lord our God; for we rest on thee, and in thy name we go against this multitude. O Lord, thou art our God; let not man prevail against thee.

So the Lord smote the Ethiopians before Asa, and before Judah; and the Ethiopians fled. — 2 Chron. 14: 2–12.

And when Asa heard . . . the prophecy of Oded the prophet, he took courage, and put away the abominable idols out of all the land of Judah and Benjamin, and out of the cities which he had taken from Mount Ephraim, and renewed the altar of the Lord that was before the porch of the Lord.

And he gathered all Judah and Benjamin, and the strangers with them out of Ephraim and Manasseh, and out of Simeon: for they fell to him out of Israel in abundance, when they saw that the Lord his God was with him. — 2 Chron. 15: 8, 9.

III.

He shall feed his flock like a shepherd: he shall gather the lambs with his arm, and carry them in his bosom. — Isa. 40: 11.

And Jesus called a little child unto him, and set him in the midst of them,

And said, Verily I say unto you, Except ye be converted, and become as little children, ye shall not enter into the kingdom of heaven.

Whosoever therefore shall humble himself as this little child, the same is greatest in the kingdom of heaven.

And whoso shall receive one such little child in my name receiveth me. — Matt. 18: 2–5.

Then were there brought unto him little children, that he should put his hands on them, and pray: and the disciples rebuked them.

But Jesus said, Suffer little children, and forbid them not, to come unto me: for of such is the kingdom of heaven.

And he laid his hands on them, and departed thence. — Matt. 19: 13–15.

So when they had dined, Jesus saith to Simon Peter, Simon, son of Jonas, lovest thou me more than these? He saith unto him, Yea, Lord; thou knowest that I love thee. He saith unto him, Feed my lambs. — John 21: 15.

IV.

Then the children of Judah came unto Joshua in Gilgal: and Caleb the son of Jephunneh the Kenezite said unto him, Thou knowest the thing that the Lord said unto Moses the man of God concerning me and thee in Kadesh-barnea.

Forty years old was I when Moses the servant of the Lord sent me from Kadesh-barnea to espy out the land; and I brought him word again as it was in mine heart.

Nevertheless my brethren that went up with me made the heart of the people melt: but I wholly followed the Lord my God.

And Moses sware on that day, saying, Surely the land whereon thy feet have trodden shall be thine inheritance, and thy children's for ever, because thou hast wholly followed the Lord my God.

And now, behold, the Lord hath kept me alive, as he said, these forty and five years, even since the Lord spake this word unto Moses, while the children of Israel wandered in the wilderness: and now, lo, I am this day fourscore and five years old.

As yet I am as strong this day as I was in the day that Moses sent me: as my strength was then, even so is my strength now, for war, both to go out, and to come in.

Now therefore give me this mountain, whereof the Lord spake in that day. — Josh. 14: 6-12.

V.

And I looked, and, lo, a Lamb stood on the mount Sion, and with him an hundred forty and four thousand, having his Father's name written in their foreheads.

And I heard a voice from heaven, as the voice of many waters, and as the voice of a great thunder: and I heard the voice of harpers harping with their harps:

And they sung as it were a new song before the throne, and before the four living creatures, and the elders: and no man could learn that song but the hundred and forty and four thousand, which were redeemed from the earth.

. . . These are they which follow the Lamb whithersoever he goeth. These were redeemed from among men, being the firstfruits unto God and to the Lamb.

And in their mouth was found no guile: for they are without fault before the throne of God. — Rev. 14: 1-5.

VI.

And Asa slept with his fathers, and died in the one and fortieth year of his reign.

And they buried him in his own sepulchres, which he had made for himself in the city of David, and laid him in the bed which was filled with sweet odours and divers kinds of spices prepared by the apothecaries' art: and they made a very great burning for him. — 2 Chron. 16: 13, 14.

Thou shalt come to thy grave in a full age, like as a shock of corn cometh in in his season. — Job 5: 26.

The hoary head is a crown of glory, if it be found in the way of righteousness. — Prov. 16: 31.

And I heard a voice from heaven saying unto me, Write, Blessed are the dead which die in the Lord from henceforth: Yea, saith the Spirit, that they may rest from their labours; and their works do follow them. — Rev. 14: 13.

VII.

The grace of our Lord Jesus Christ be with you all. Amen. — Rev. 22: 21.

The following extracts from the addresses given, appropriately find place here : —

From the address of Rev. A. E. Dunning, D.D., representing the Congregational Sunday-School and Publishing Society : —

THE heathen proverb, "Whom the gods love die young," has been Christianized and transfigured by our father and brother. After eighty-four years he died young, and during his life had peculiar evidences that he was beloved of God. To the last he enjoyed his life. His thoughts were as vigorous and his step as elastic as when he was a boy, and to the last his trust in God was as simple and serene and happy as that of a child.

Fifty-four years ago last month he was chosen General Agent of the Massachusetts Sabbath-School Society. At that time he already was an experienced Sabbath-school worker. A few months before that Society was organized he was ordained to the ministry of the gospel. His public life has more than covered the history of the Society, and, excepting for the first two years, he has been identified with it during the whole time until now, and much of that time as one of its chief executive officers. The Society has changed its name again and again to accommodate itself to its increasing responsibilities, but his name has remained associated with it from the first to the last.

During his long life the most wonderful advances in history in the most wonderful country of the world have taken place, and he has been associated with them in their broadest and highest relations. In the interest of his Society he traversed the west when railroads had not penetrated it, and when the regions beyond were still unexplored and unknown. He has seen the silent prairies that he crossed teem with busy life, and upon them he has beheld cities spring up peopled by generations of men and women whom he has helped to teach, to make brave defenders of their country, and to be faithful citizens of the kingdom of our Lord Jesus Christ.

He has continually associated himself with children. Two themes have been on his mind for many, many years: First, The Bible and Its Study; and how naturally do the sentences from the Holy Word, as they have been read, associate themselves with his name and life, as a sweet and solemn anthem where words are set to music, filling us all with a grateful sense of worship! And next, Children and their Religious Training. He talked with children continually. He founded *The Well-Spring*, and for forty years was its editor, much of the time with a regular audience of 60,000 children. He never was installed over a local parish, but perhaps there is not a minister living who has spoken to so many people at such impressible periods in their lives as he. Think of it! a whole generation has grown up to maturity who can remember him in their childhood as the tall man with the kindly countenance crowned with snow-white hair.

His love for his work did not wane with age. Four years ago, when he had reached the fiftieth anniversary of his association with this Society, its Board of Managers voted to relieve him of further labor, to continue his salary, and to ask him to address churches and Sunday-schools and other assemblies only as his strength and leisure should allow. Yet he would not give up his work. It was to him what play is to a boy. He loved it with all his heart. There are thousands and thousands of people, all the way from ocean to ocean, who will remember him with pious enthusiasm, love, and esteem, and a multitude more in that country to which he has departed, where there is no more sea. I think that the boys and girls of three weeks ago listened to him as eagerly as did those other boys and girls of half a century since, most of whom have vanished from the earth.

Only a few weeks ago I said to him: "You ought to rest. These are cold winter days ; wait till spring." And with a twinkle in his eye he told me that every Sunday was engaged away into June. So I repeat that he has transfigured the proverb, " Whom the gods love die young." After such a rarely long and useful life, closed with a sickness so brief that it seemed no more than the summons from the chariot in waiting to bear him to his permanent home, may we not look up into the skies admiringly and gratefully, and say, as children and brethren of him who has been so long amongst us, " We give thee joy, our father and our brother ! "

From the address of Mr. Charles W. Hill, representing the Congregational Superintendents' Union : —

WE are drawing near to the end of a very remarkable century, remarkable in material and in spiritual things, but for nothing to be remembered more than for the systematic study of the Bible, which has been its crowning glory. In this great work our revered friend, whose name we take upon our lips with loving affection, was a pioneer. Born in the very dawn of the century, entering upon this great work while it was still young, he has spent the strength of his manhood in it.

Mr. Bullard was eminently fitted for the work to which he was called. There was about him a gentle sprightliness which always attracts children ; there was at his command a wealth of illustration which very few have equaled and none surpassed. There was in him a youthfulness of spirit which never grew old ; there was a buoyant hopefulness which boys and girls always love to meet. He was loved by more who are and have been children than any other man of our times.

The Superintendents' Union, which I have the privilege to-day of representing, welcomed him in its very earliest years to an honored and honorary place in its membership. His words voiced our thanks during all the last years of our gatherings. I do not know how at first he came to be called our chaplain, but it fell naturally to him to invoke a blessing upon the food of which we were about to partake, and the exercise was always an uplifting one ; we were always brought nearer to the great Source of all good by his words, which always came from his heart. He was to us, I might say, both father and brother. Rarely is it that one combines both relations so completely and fully as did he. We looked up to him with veneration for what he had done and for what he was ; and he sat down beside us as a brother sits by the side of brother. There was no air of superiority about him ; there was almost the opposite. It was an inspiration to meet him. It was an attraction to the Union to know that Asa Bullard would be at its meeting.

There was nothing about him of the pessimism of old age. He looked about with a faithful Christian's hope. We would have detained him a little longer if we could, but it would have been for our own sakes and to his loss. Each of us, if we might, would have been to him what Elisha was to the great prophet. We would have gone over Jordan with him, and walked and talked with him until the chariot should have descended; and then we should have been constrained to cry out, as did the younger prophet, "My father, my father, the chariots of Israel and the horsemen thereof!" And we would have made of him Elisha's request, that a double portion of his spirit might fall upon us. We do humbly wait upon God, beseeching him that the mantle of our father may fall upon us, bringing with it that double portion of his spirit that shall send us forth to our work equipped with something of his Christian, hopeful zeal.

We shall go on no three days' journey, as did the foolish sons of the prophets, upon the mountains and through the valleys looking for him. He is not here; he is gone up on high. Wide have opened the pearly gates to admit this conquering hero. Many and many are the children who have welcomed him home. Loud, I believe, have the hallelujahs rung through the heavenly arches as he has made his triumphal way. And yet he has triumphed not in himself, but in Jesus Christ his Lord and Master, and at the foot of his throne he has cast all of his laurels down. This beloved form which has gone in and out before us, imparting an inspiration to higher, nobler, and better things, we shall see no more until the sea gives up its dead. But his spirit remains, his work goes on, and through this and through all coming ages there shall be an accumulation of influences set in motion by him which shall bless this and all lands.

From the address of Rev. A. H. Plumb, D.D., representing the pastors of Boston and vicinity : —

In our father Bullard was illustrated in a remarkable manner the beautiful simplicity of a truly religious character. He was a perfect child to the last in the utter guilelessness of his spirit. Personal ambition, self-seeking, a desire to shine among men, were motives unknown to him. He sought to win the hearts of children; he sought to win souls to Christ; he sought to unfold the riches of God's Word. In this, doubtless, he was assisted largely by those for whom he labored. The children did a great deal for Mr. Bullard. It is a great privilege for a Christian worker to be especially associated with the young, for it keeps one young. It kept him so. There was great native simplicity in his character, and being with children so much kept him always guileless and childlike. Having the children before him continuously, Mr. Bullard more and more assimilated to them, and in that period of life when many are apt to grow bitter in their feelings and to wear a sad countenance, the sunny faces of the children illuminated his own, and his spirit responded.

Then, too, it gives a man directness and efficiency in speech to be dealing always with children. For their attention can not be held and permanent and effective impressions be made unless these qualities reign in speech. Consequently, our brother, as many of us pastors had occasion to see of late years, was constantly improving in the directness and efficiency of his speech. There are few men who can give a better address upon the Bible than he could, and largely because his address was marked with these qualities. The children did a good deal for him, and he did a great deal for the children.

What a magnificent thing it is to stand for over half a century, as he stood, at the fountains of religious character, turning the streams at the fountain head in the right way! There are multitudes every-where who remember and cherish the little things that he has said. Here is a letter written years ago by him, a few lines of which I will read. It was written on a Christmas morning here at Cambridgeport to a family of children : —

"I remember, my dear boys, with much interest, the perfect manner in which you recited the catechism to your mother, at the time of my visit a few years ago. I trust you will ever find those important truths you so thoroughly stored in your minds in early life a great help and blessing to you. Your dear parents have this morning presented you with a book far more valuable than that excellent catechism. It is the sacred Book, which, through faith in Jesus Christ, made young Timothy wise unto salvation. It is the best book in the world. You will find it the most attractive book you ever possessed."

Then he gives directions very fully as to reading it, advising them to read a portion at a time, quite a large portion, and then he says : "You take the history of Joseph and read it, and if you can go through it without the tears starting, you will do better than I can." And then he exhorts them to make it "the lamp to their feet and the light of their path." Now, for a man to be remembered all over the country by thousands of men upon whom in their youth he has thus laid his hand is a very great privilege ; it is a very high service.

His life was successful, also, because it was a very long one. The Duke of Wellington's life was called very successful, because he had opportunities that fall to few men. God kept this man in such serenity of spirit, such equable temper, and such firm religious health that the years passed him lightly by, so that wherever he went of late years there were strong men rising up and greeting him, and recalling the time when he was speaking to them in their youth of Christ and the Bible. I am called upon to speak here as one of the older ministers in this region, but Mr. Bullard was making public addresses before I was born. Think of the privilege of standing for so many years in Christ's name! Think of the host of his spiritual children he has met in the world to which he has gone !

I must not close without a word as to the manner in which he has borne the ministerial character. We have never had to blush for this man as a member of our association and as a representative minister going through the country. No minister has ever felt any thing but honored that he belonged to a profession which this man so illustrated and adorned. A man once showed me an infidel paper, in which the histories of all the wicked things that ministers had ever done, so far as they could be obtained, were displayed and detailed. They were raked together from all over the country, and I suppose that there may have been fifty men who were thus exposed, and perhaps more. But say there were ten times fifty, five hundred, or eight hundred, what would that amount to? Who can judge of ministers by that? Dr. Dorchester's recent book tells us that there are 83,854 evangelical Protestant ministers in the United States. Suppose you show that fifty or a hundred of them go astray, what has that to do with ministerial character? That is to be determined by the unsullied lives of the great majority. The great mass of ministers are noble and good men. And this man has worn the ministerial character and name and reputation, and not only has kept them unsullied, but has adorned them. As we think of the long fellowship we have had together, and of renewing that fellowship in the bright world to come, we say, Farewell for a season, benignant, blessed, godly man !

From the address of Rev. Alexander McKenzie, D.D., representing neighbors and friends : —

IT seems fitting that a moment should be taken at the close of these services in which the neighbors and friends of our father who has "fallen upon sleep" should add their word of respect and affection. Yet our thoughts are so much quicker and so much better than our words, that the longer we wait the more impossible it seems to say any thing that shall add to the thought and feelings which are in our hearts. I am sure that we who stood very near to him as his fellow-citizens in this town appreciate these tributes of respect which are brought to him from without,

His was a remarkably favored life, a remarkably successful life. It had in it certain elements that are not altogether common, that are far from universal, and which, when you find them together, will always make up a life of honor and of usefulness and of happiness. He was extremely favored in this, that he was in the right place. Of all the callings which it is possible for a man to enter, he had the one to which he was precisely fitted. He had, again, this qualification for his office, that he could enjoy it because he was fitted for it, and because it was a life that brought him continually new life and new thought from the new, fresh life which he was touching; for if it be true that to-day is as yesterday, and that which has been is that which is to be, still nothing ever becomes old to one who lives with children, and life never becomes monotonous to one who walks among the flowers. Every day is a new day, as if there never had been a day before it, and this was enough to keep his life fresh. Then the wonderful privilege of being able to speak to the children, to teach them what had been taught him in his childhood, what he had learned in his youth, what he had gained for himself in his manhood; to look into their bright faces; to put the impress of his fatherly hand and to breathe the breath of his fatherly wisdom upon their young lives, — this wonderful privilege was his.

God gave him another trait which is rare. I wish it were not so rare; the lack of it makes so many men unhappy in their last years. He had the remarkable gift that he could consent to the changes of life. A man who can see another take his place has learned the hardest lesson of life; has shown his fitness for his work when he can give it over into the hands of others. I do not think that our dear friend always approved every thing which is done in these new days. I think that there was many a sigh for the old Society, which he had known from its infancy. I think he always loved that long name, which be pronounced as though it were one syllable. I think that he saw with something of dismay the turning away from its simple methods into the broader work which opened before it. I think that he saw with delight the going back to the methods of his youth — the Sunday-school, and the children taking the places which they had in some measure yielded to the new interests. But he consented to changes. He saw somebody else edit *The Well-Spring*, the hardest trial of his life, I suppose. But he saw it, and yet kept his hand and his heart in *The Well-Spring* still. He saw new secretaries take up his work; he kept his place as Secretary still. He saw other men speaking for the Society here and there; he kept speaking for the Society still. You might call him Honorary Secretary, or what you would, his salary might be more or less, he was still true through all changes to the work of his youth, to the work of his life. That marvelously strange lesson which so few of us can learn, to grow old gracefully, and to bless the man that takes our place, he had learned, and, as we look upon it, it is almost the proudest honor of his life.

While he kept very closely to his work all his life, he had side interests which were of concern to him. He was extremely fond of flowers. He lived in the garden and forest. He loved the flowers and he loved the trees. He followed into nature the great Teacher, who was its Creator, and he considered the lily, not alone how beautiful it is, but how it speaks to us of its Creator. He saw in it the Saviour's care and the Saviour's love, and the perfume that was exhaled from it was to him but the breath of the loving providence in which he trusted. I never can forget, it comes back to me now, what I heard him say once when I was a little boy: "Children," said he, "if you were going to make a present of a flower to your father, you would not bring him a rose full-blown and perfect, whose leaves would presently drop off, but you would bring him a bud. Children, don't think that by-and-by, when you are men, you will give your hearts to God, but give them in the bud, and let them open before him." That was one way in which he used the flowers, making his garden a parable from which he could teach those divine lessons of love, which considers the lily and the child who loves the lily.

There is one thing more which comes to me as characterizing him, and that is the marvelous enjoyment he had of every thing. He had open eyes, seeing every thing, hearing every thing. I scarcely ever met him, when he did not tell me something he had seen the day before, or heard the last Sunday. When he went away it was to bring home something. It was a wonderful trip he made to Europe a few years ago, wonderful in its beginning through the shipwreck, and then in the great convention he attended in England. Then the strange things he saw, the interesting sights and great men he looked upon; how over and over again he told us about things that you and I, perhaps, might never have seen. He seemed to have walked the world with his eyes open to every thing, gathering up and remembering, with that genius for seeing things that ought to be seen, and with that greater genius for remembering what ought to be told.

When I think of him, as I have for these few last days, I have not been able to think of him as gone. As he comes to my mind and I try to think of him as beyond the stars somewhere, it always comes to me in this way: I suppose we think of different people in heaven in different relations, and think of them in different occupations. It seems to me that Asa Bullard in heaven is seeing a great many new things. Think how eager he is! He has seen the amethyst and chrysoprase and sardonyx that are in the jeweled walls. He has seen the golden streets; he knows how wide they are. He has heard the harpers; he has listened to the angels. If it be possible, he has seen Saint Paul; he has seen Saint John; he has looked up into that radiant face which comes to us as the highest revelation of all imagined glory, for we shall be like Him when we see him, because we shall see him as he is. I like to think of this. My dear friend, I love to think how you are enjoying heaven!

I wish that he could come back some Sunday afternoon and say: "Children, I want to tell you how those walls look; I want to tell you about the harps; and I want to tell you about the dear Lord!" I do not know what change has come to him. He was the first man who told me that when we die we do not become angels. I was brought up to believe that every body who was good became an angel. He said: "No, children, no, we do not become angels; we are nothing but men and women after we are gone." I think of him as being a man still; I do not know what changes may come, but I hope they will not change Asa Bullard very much. I want to see that tall form and that kindly face. I think, if it were left to me, I should not change it at all; a little of the weariness might be taken off, perhaps, yet it was that weariness that gave the glory to his spirit and life. I hope his hair will be white there. I want to see the twinkle of his eyes. It seems to me that when I see him, — I picture myself going towards him, and he is waiting while I am talking with Saint Paul for a moment, waiting quietly, and as soon as I turn he says: "Come with me, and I will show you the Bride, the Lamb's wife." Then he will show me the pure river of water of life proceeding out of the throne of God, and the glory which is forever in that city, where they never shut the gates, where the sun never goes down, where there is no night, and where there is no sorrow forever and forever. O my dear friend, how you are enjoying heaven! God bless you in that glory! Thou art worthy; thou art worthy of the light of eternal day, for thou wast a disciple of Him who said, "Because I live, ye shall live also."

The services were closed with a touching prayer by the pastor, and then the remains were taken to Mount Auburn for interment.

To those who know the facts concerning Mr. Bullard and his life-work, it is manifest that he has very inadequately represented them in his autobiography. He has not written down that which was the most valuable and for which he is the most honored. It is doubtful whether he himself sufficiently realized what they were so that he could have done so. It is difficult for any one to look at himself and his acts in such a way as to get things in right perspectives. But even if he rightly estimated his relations to the work in which he was engaged, his deep humility of character would have prevented him from putting that estimate before others. Whenever he approached any thing like a summary of what he had accomplished, his pen sensitively was guided away from characterizing it in any way. The reports of some men are larger than their deeds, but he was one who did more than he ever told. He has left it to others to say what value shall be placed upon his work.

Already others are appraising his labors at their true

worth, and are rating them far higher than his own modesty ever would have dreamed of placing them. While he still was wavering between life and death, the Boston Congregational Superintendents' Union passed the following minute : —

"*Voted*, That an effort be made throughout the country to raise a Trust Fund of One Hundred Thousand Dollars, to be known as the ASA BULLARD MEMORIAL FUND, the income of which shall be used in the missionary work of the Congregational Sunday-School and Publishing Society."

It was thought that the communication to him of this proposed effort would help Mr. Bullard to get well, or at least to cheer his last hours. But he was beyond the reception of any messages, no matter how full of affection they might be. He died without knowing what was intended by the Union.

A committee of seven was appointed to carry out the purpose expressed in the resolution. Of that committee Mr. C. W. Carter is chairman, Mr. F. P. Shumway, Jr., is secretary, and Mr. W. H. Emerson, 40 Central Street, Boston, is treasurer.

It is not the design of the Union that the raising of this fund shall in any way interfere with the contributions now coming into the Society, upon which it is depending for the means necessary to carry on its missionary work. Its members, indeed, earnestly deprecate any diversion of those contributions to this object, for that would for the present, at least, cripple the Society which they, in honoring its departed servant, seek to help. They seek to make the subscriptions to the fund individual rather than to have them given collectively by Sunday-schools and churches.

The committee is already vigorously at work. Circulars

have been issued, and certificates of subscription have been prepared. An engraved receipt is to be given to every one contributing the sum of twenty-five cents, while a card certificate bearing the autograph and an excellent likeness of Mr. Bullard engraved from a recent photograph will be sent to all of those who contribute one dollar or more. It is expected that some will contribute as high as a thousand dollars or even more. There will be many whose warm affection will not allow themselves to be limited to a small amount. Before the arrangements are complete, the responses are beginning to come in. The prospects for success seem hopeful. At a memorial meeting of the Boston Superintendents' Union, eighteen hundred dollars was subscribed by the members present toward the fund. The children of fifty years ago, the children of twenty-five years since, and the children of to-day will raise the memorial.

And such a memorial will better fit the saint for whom it is intended than a stately monument in Mount Auburn. His work meant every thing to him, and by this memorial the work will go on. It will be as if the folded hands should again resume their labors, and his presence for ages be felt in the homes that are yet to be. By this, he, being dead, will yet speak, and speak most effectively, to the oncoming generations of children. In this way shall his last prayer be most fully answered: "GOD BLESS US ALL!"

www.ingramcontent.com/pod-product-compliance
Lightning Source LLC
Chambersburg PA
CBHW020120030726

47498CB00006B/2204